Sleeping Patterns

J.R. Crook

Legend Press
Independent Book Publisher

Legend Press Ltd, 2 London Wall Buildings,
London EC2M 5UU
info@legend-paperbooks.co.uk
www.legendpress.co.uk

British Library Cataloguing in Publication Data available.

ISBN 978-1-9087755-2-8

*All characters, other than those clearly in the public domain, and
place names, other than those well-established such as towns and
cities, are ficticious and any resemblance is purely coincidental.*

Set in Times
Printed by Lightning Source, Milton Keynes, UK

Cover designed by Gudrun Jobst
www.yotedesign.com

Legend Press

Independent Book Publisher

Dedicated to the memory of the author

A BRIEF INTRODUCTION
By Annelie Strandli

Hello. My name is Annelie Strandli, or to my friends, Grethe. I am a character in the novel you are about to read, but also a real person, a person who does not know what to say. As you may have already gathered from the dedication, the author, J.R. Crook, is dead. I knew Jamie well, or at least, I once thought I did. Some years ago now, we lived together in a residence for students in South London. It was the building within which this novel is set.

I feel it is essential for you to know a few things before you start. For some time prior to the author's death, I had been receiving envelopes from him through the post, each one containing a piece of an untitled story. There were fifteen pieces in total and each took me entirely by surprise. They arrived in a strange order and were written in a tone I had almost forgotten, but instantly recognised. I had no idea why he was sending them to me, because at that point we had not been in contact for years. I read each piece carefully, trying to locate any meaning that might be hidden between the lines. However, it was not until shortly after his death, once the last piece had arrived, that I came to understand what the purpose of his writing had been.

On behalf of the author, I have pieced together his work and am now presenting it in the order I first received it. It is offered to you here as a work of fiction, even though I have not changed any of the names of the people in it. I have also given it a title, *Sleeping Patterns*, which I feel is appropriate.

Thank you for reading.

Grethe

SLEEPING PATTERNS

A Story in Fifteen Pieces

By J.R. Crook

5

November.

Tomorrow, for feeling unable to resist doing so, Annelie Strandli would ascend the stairwell with cautious footsteps. The hallway she would reach on the seventh floor would be dimly lit and grey. She would walk along it and from underneath each of the closed doors she passed by, feel rushes of cold air on her bare ankles that would make her shiver.

It would be for her curiosity, for her need to discover more about *him*, that she would approach his room at the end of the hallway and open it without knocking. She would be seeking evidence of his writings, of any imagined words that he may have committed to a page. She would be hoping that small fictions and understated truths were there for her to find. She would be fancying the image of the writer's hands, like those of an illusionist's, revealing to her all manner of things invisible before.

Everything would be as she expected it to be: the door would be unlocked and she would only need to push it; the room would be empty and she would only need to cross it; *he* would be elsewhere and she would only need to remember it. She would have an idea about where his writings might be found, should any actually exist. She would approach his wooden desk at the far side of the room and push aside the piles of things he would always leave on top.

She would not feel the reservations she had thought she would. Her conscience would stay strangely quiet. She would be considering it essential that she understood more about the person whom, in just over six weeks, she had grown so quickly fond of. She would be hoping that in the quiet gaps between his words and in the spaces behind his pages, his truth would be there for her to find. She would envisage signposts being noted and puzzle-pieces being found and the comfort she would feel afterwards, for knowing *him* a little deeper.

There would be the sound of rain hitting the windows. Briefly, she would pause to glance outside and follow the rainwater as it tumbled down the sides of the opposing building. Then, to deny herself enough time to change her mind, she would quickly flip open the lid of the desk and reveal an inner compartment. She would smile, having been proven right. Inside, lying awkwardly upon a bed of cigarette ash, there would be papers, pages of typed writing. Then, without any hesitation, she would sit down and allow herself to drift carelessly into the beginning of the story…

One

Once upon a time, upon a day that might have easily been forgotten, there was a boy who was dreaming about nothing in particular. He was slumping idly in his seat, having allowed his mind to depart into a dangerous sleep. In the background of his dream, he began to hear a familiar voice, shortly followed by the sensation of being shaken by the shoulder.

'Hey! It's time to go home. Or would you prefer to be left here alone?'

Arriving back from what felt like a great distance away, the dreamer began to show signs of life.

'Come on, it really is time for us to go now… '

He heard the sounds of the wind in the trees, the creaking of an old window frame, the banging of a door that had been caught by a draught. He opened his eyes and looked around. The room was empty; it had been deserted immediately after the bell had rung.

'Let's go… '

Finally, Boy One rose from his chair, rubbed his eyes and then followed his friend out into the hallway.

'Is the lesson really over already?' he asked.

'Yes and before you ask - he didn't notice you,' Boy Two answered, pre-empting his friend's next question, 'or at least, I don't think he did. But maybe Mr Letters has become so used to your habits that he no longer cares to do anything about it… '

Together they walked down the steps at the front of the school and onto the pavement. Boy One watched as his friend paced ahead and listened to the sound made by a lone pencil as it bounced around his empty rucksack.

'Hey! Wait for me!' he called out, seeing that Boy Two had reached the entrance to the park without him.

'Come on,' Boy Two shouted back, 'why are you so slow?'

'Sorry,' replied Boy One, as he quickly jogged the distance between them. 'I'm still feeling quite sleepy. I did only just wake up, after all.'

'It's fine. Only, can we get going now… we're going to Old Man's today, aren't we?'

'Of course we are. Isn't that what lunch money's for?'

Boy Two grinned, but then turned to his friend and sensing that something was not quite right, commented: 'You're different today, somehow. What's wrong with you?'

There was not so much as anything wrong with Boy One, rather his priorities were opposite to what is generally considered right. He was a dreamer. To him, it seemed as if the people he was surrounded by – his parents, his peers, the residents of the small town where he lived – all held the act of dreaming in little regard. They had all consigned dreaming to the small hours, to times of nocturnal abandon. They only dreamt in secluded places, in blanketed corners. They paid little, if any attention toward the theatre of the naked mind and preferred, upon daybreak, to forget their times spent wandering in the clouds.

For Boy One however, the arena of sleep was wide, and the dreams it contained were without walls or recipe. He believed there to be no quilted nest, or daytime routine that could ever stop him from dreaming whenever he pleased. The difference between Boy One and his peers was that he always contested his alarm clock and allowed his dreaming to overflow into the daylight hours.

'Nothing,' he replied. 'I was just thinking about something, that's all.'

'Well, I think you need to stop sleeping in class... '

'Hmm... '

Boy One stopped to tighten a loose shoelace that had been blackened by the underside of his shoe, then looked up and added: 'By the way, I wasn't just sleeping - I was dreaming.'

'Okay, okay,' Boy Two rolled his eyes, growing impatient,

'and do you want to know what you missed whilst you were, er, away?'

'Of course.'

As they moved on, the shop came into view; it was at the far side of the park and felt magnetic.

'It was about power and economics and the rules of success...'

'So?'

'... and something called Globalisation...'

They finally reached the shop and pushed against the door. As they entered, the bronze bell that was hanging above them rang.

'That's a big word.'

'Yep. Glo-bal-is-a-tion,' repeated Boy Two as he pulled his money out from his pocket. 'I think it's some kind of movement - it's the new Enlightenment, apparently.'

The two boys each opened a small paper bag and began to fill them with sweets from the containers on the shelves.

'So when I woke up, why were all of those names written on the blackboard?'

'Oh yes, they were the names of powerful men. Their job is to keep the balance of power in the world weighed in their own – and therefore our – favour. I didn't recognise any of them from TV, but apparently they're very important men.'

'Is that what Mr Letters said?'

'Yes. He admires them. He said that successful people should be respected. He pointed to their names with his stick, over and over again, as if we couldn't already see them. You know, I'd like to be great like that someday...'

'Why?' Boy One asked, rolling up the top of his paper bag so that its contents could not escape by mistake. 'So that you can have your name poked at with a stick by the likes of Mr

Letters? What's so great about that?'

Then suddenly, from the counter behind them, came an eruption: 'Devils! Those aren't men, they're devils... '

Old Man liked nothing more than leaning over the counter of his shop, receiving pennies and paper bags and speaking about things that made him shake. He considered himself a nameless spokesman against modern dross and cultural dictation. Despite suffering from an outward sense of idealism that was wholly departed from the actualities by which he lived, he used to be, and to a certain extent remained, a very clever man. He was an academic without education and a self-professed theoretical sculptor of alternate social and cultural systems. In between serving his customers in his sweet shop, he would spend his days formulating ideas about the things he was most impassioned by, and then recount them to anyone willing to listen. He desperately hoped to see the day when the moral universe would shun the relentless lusts and wants of the powerful few – who he loathed, above all else – in favour of comfort and peace for all.

Old Man used to be a prolific writer and therefore, his understanding of Time, and its habits, was not based upon clock strokes, but rather the words he had written. For him, the past, and more importantly the future, were certain. It was for this reason that Boy One viewed him as a figure of aspiration. Upon sugary afternoons, he would listen as Old Man threw forth wild, stabbing words of crazed beauty, sometimes coherent and sometimes not, but enough of which he had to flood a library.

'Erm, I'm sorry about that, boys... '

They handed their paper bags over the counter to be

weighed.

'... but I couldn't help overhearing what you were just discussing... '

They heard the rusty drawer of the cash register sliding open.

'... so please, allow me to tell you something... '

They heard their coins being dropped into the tray.

'... something about Big Business and notions of global authority... '

Pausing for a moment, Old Man rested his arms upon the counter and leant forward. For sensing that they were about to be subjected to another one of his theories, Boy One and Boy Two shared a knowing glance, unrolled the tops of their paper bags and filled their mouths with fizzy shapes.

'The world is only as big as the men in the skyscrapers,' he began. 'Doing business in the sky makes the devils feel as if they're masters of kingdoms below... '

The two recipients had begun to nod along with the speaker: Boy One encouragingly so and Boy Two only politely so.

'... yet, it is this very fondness for heights that could prove to be their downfall... '

The sweets tasted good; they were mostly of the sour kind.

'Elevators. I've thought long and hard about it and have reached the conclusion that elevators might be the key to the undoing of Big Business. Allow me to explain, boys. Now, we all know that in the absence of elevators, a businessman would be too lazy to climb countless staircases instead. Therefore, we can deduce that without elevators, these men would essentially be unable to reach their celebrated heights and unable to make their high-rise decisions... '

Behind them, the door blew open and the bronze bell rang. A splash of brown leaves swept across the shop floor.

'... and so my theory is this - if one could stop all of the elevators, one could effectively halt the march of Globalisation. You see, boys, what if for all this time, elevators have been the modern world's hidden remedy for itself?'

Outside the wind was blowing in circles. As they walked home, they had to shield their eyes from spinning dirt and leaves.

'What is it?' Boy One finally asked his friend, who, for some considerable time since leaving the shop, had been shaking his head.

'It's Old Man - he's losing it, isn't he?'

'I don't know.'

'Well that theory of his made no sense at all.'

'Perhaps. But I still like his words, regardless of whether or not they make any sense... '

Boy Two shrugged and began to kick a small stone along the pavement ahead.

'... I mean, his mind must be fizzing like his sweets. He must have thoughts bubbling up to the surface all the time,' Boy One continued. 'I wonder what his dreams are like. I bet they're busy, really busy, and full of new ideas that are dashing around all over the place...'

'Nah,' Boy Two interrupted, 'I don't think so.'

'Why?'

'Because, my friend, you're overlooking the fact that old people probably only dream about one thing. That is, if they still dream at all.'

'And what's that?'

Boy Two stopped and opened the gate to his home.

'The past,' he replied, walking away from his friend. 'It's like how young people always dream about the future... '

She would look up and take a deep breath. The rain would have stopped hitting the glass. The room would be silent and it would make her feel nervous. In a quick glance towards the door, she would picture *him* appearing at any moment, like a phantom, and destroying all of her secret plans.

The pages would still be in her hands and lightly shaking. There would be a few lines remaining for her to read, but before finishing them, she would stand up and return to the desk. She would peer into the inner compartment, hoping to see another page lying in there, one that she had somehow overlooked before. But for then, at least, there would be nothing else for her to find: there would be only a pile of cigarette ash.

He waved to his friend and watched him disappear behind the front door of his house. It was the end of another day.

And then, as Boy One began to walk the final distance to his own home, he did so with an unusual smile. It was true, he thought, as he began kicking the small stone that his friend had started before: he did always dream about the future...

1

September.

His voice had sounded strange, like a voice always does when there is no-one else around to hear it. If it were not for the boxes in the corner, nor the rustling of his feet against the greyish carpet, nor the memory of how his words had just been lost in space, the empty room may as well have never existed.

From below came the sound of a passing train. He watched from the window as it rolled past and caught sight of a few people inside, swaying in their seats to the rhythm of the tracks. He then turned back to the pile of cardboard boxes, to the stack of things with which he would claim the room, and began to unpack them. He opened the box he considered most important first and assembled its contents; so that a record could be played; so that the trains would disappear; so that the room would be in colour, at least.

I, meanwhile in my room, had started to hear unfamiliar sounds. Beyond the book I was reading, I could hear footsteps pacing around in circles. Then there was music.

So I moved my ear closer to the wall…

The record crackled, waiting to be turned over. His homely things, for lack of shelves, were now standing in hastily arranged towers that sometimes threatened to fall. He sat upon the bed and it made a crunching sound; the mattress was coated in a thick plastic film. He rolled a cigarette and, entrusting himself to its powers of distraction, lit it with the last match he had in his pocket. He wished not to think about what kinds of things his new bed must have seen.

He got up again and went over to the far side of the room where, beneath two large windows, there was an old wooden desk. He squashed his smallest finger into the rusty keyhole on the front and looked out through the windows. The view was obscured on one side by thick tree branches. Then, resting his arms upon the wooden desktop, he leant forward to press his crown against the glass and peered down at the deep concrete grooves that ran the length of the building. He noted that due to the city lights below, the night sky appeared more orange than black.

Down a hole he had found in the top-left corner of the desk, he discarded his finished cigarette and, as he moved back, blew his last stream of smoke toward the window. He observed how the smoke crashed against the glass, spread out like a wave and broke at the frame.

Over the next couple of days, I would often hear mysterious footsteps outside my room. I wanted to know whose feet they were. I would often try to open my door at the right moment and catch them. But I would always be too slow.

He, meanwhile, heavily clothed for the cold autumn air, would have started to venture into the nearby town. The area had been built upon a celebrated past for which he did not care and yet, he liked it. The building where he lived was located in the eastern region of the town – for it felt like an independent town, even though it was really just another piece of the wider city – and was only a brief walk away from its centre.

Whenever at home, he would spend much of his time quietly walking along the hallway between his room and the stairwell. He would not see much sign of anyone else. In fact, he would often believe he was the only person there.

*

I placed down the book I had been reading for days.

I looked in the mirror above the sink in the corner.

I calmed my messy hair with splashes of water from the tap.

I stroked the sharp stubble on my chin with the palm of my hand.

I took a deep breath and then left my room.

He looked outside. It was hardly the 'Stunning Panoramic Views' that the glossy brochure had promised him. The opposing building looked as if it had once been a Victorian school or institution of some sort. It was empty, but for the stones that had been thrown by local kids through its windows and the ivy that had grown to cover every inch of its brickwork. He could also see, in the half-distance, a hospital that had long-since been deserted, which he imagined smelt strongly of moss and ghosts.

After spending an hour or two in the park, he had climbed the seven floors of the concrete stairwell, rather than using the elevator. He did not trust the elevator; with the exception of a small grid-lined window, stained yellow with decades of dust, it was a solid box that regularly – and more often than not on quiet nights – took captive the unwary user.

I raised a fist.

Toward the source of an abrupt sound, he turned and stared, quickly discarding the tiresome magazine he had been about to flick through. He opened the door and the smoke, which had been lingering in swirls about the ceiling, was pulled into the hallway by a cold draught.

When I saw him, I said this: Hello, my name is Jamie Crook. I used to live in your room.

It began as one of those compulsory greetings, a necessary moment of nicety, where one deciphers subtleties from amidst the politeness and begins to calculate of the other.

He pushed back the door and stood aside.

'Berry Walker,' he replied with a handshake. 'Are we neighbours?'

I talked with him long into the evening. We got to know each other by smoking cigarettes and leaning back on chairs. He reminded me of myself, and of how little I had changed since arriving the year before:

I too had left the countryside in order to study.

I too had been curious and for the first time in a city by myself.

I too had not known how to say things to girls.

I too had lacked money, and the ferocious qualities one needs to get some these days.

11

April.

Annelie Strandli looked outside; the city was wet and wrapped in a mist so low that the glass towers in the distance, save the flashing light at the peak of the tallest one, were hidden almost entirely. She turned back around and lit the remains of an unfinished cigarette. Even though it was the middle of the afternoon, her room seemed darker than usual, as if through some wound in the outer wall the mist was bleeding in.

'I cannot recall the last time I saw you without Berry Walker,' said her friend, Catrina Bloodly, who was leafing through Grethe's sketchbook on the bed, whilst an imaginary camera, which she always acted as if she was being followed by, filmed everything from overhead. 'Where is he?'

Grethe knelt down beside a pile of freshly washed clothes and began to sort through them. Shortly, by the feeling of its fabric between her hands, a particular blouse reminded her of Home – of her mother's cooking drifting up the stairs, of her family's dog encircling her legs, of affectionate hands moving about her body – and into it she became lost, leaving her cigarette to burn ever nearer to her fingers.

A thin black line of smoke wove towards the ceiling. Grethe looked down; the cigarette had fallen from her hand and landed on the white blouse, lying delicately folded upon her lap. She quickly retrieved the cigarette and dropped it into a nearby glass of water, then grasped the spot between her two fingers where, at the end of her reflections, she had just allowed herself to be absent-mindedly burned.

'Grethe! What happened?'

To dilute the smell of the smouldered fabric with cold air, Catrina Bloodly, from her cross-legged position upon the bed, turned around and opened the window. As she did so, Grethe imagined that she could see rushing in, like floodwater into a riverside home, the mist from outside, to fill her room and to choke her lungs.

'I stopped to recall the smell of my mother's cooking drifting up the stairs,' she caught her breath to explain. 'Only, my cigarette did not.'

Grethe flung the ruined blouse, which had been a Christmas gift from her father, into a corner and then went over to the sink. The water that ran from the tap was lukewarm and did little to appease her fingers, but she held them beneath it nonetheless.

She continued: 'Anyway, Catrina, I didn't answer your question: I don't know where Berry is, although I shouldn't think he's too far away. After all, he's taking me out to a restaurant this evening… '

'Why would he do that?'

'He said there's something important we need to talk about... '

Although Grethe waited for her to, Catrina did not reply; she had returned to the sketchbook – her imaginary camera peering over her shoulder, her index finger poised to turn the next page – and was leaning forward, squinting, no longer listening and trying to read. Grethe did not repeat herself, but instead stopped to notice how long it had taken for the sound of her own voice to disappear. Although her room was always quite empty, for she had few possessions to fill it with, it felt emptier than usual; it always did whenever Berry Walker was not there. Upon the bedside chair, her old typewriter, which she had treasured since childhood, was occupying the place where he could normally be found.

'No, I give up!' Catrina finally shouted, closing the sketchbook. 'There's a page in here that Berry wrote for you, Grethe, and no matter how hard I try, I can't make any sense of it! Can he not write something that's readable?'

Now it was Grethe's turn to not reply; she was too busy looking forward to that night, like she did to every night. In her nocturnal room everything was always as it should be; her clothes, bundled together, would be pushed into hidden spaces; her ashtray, still warm, would be smouldering weakly; her books and papers, strewn across every surface, would be stained with the rings left by careless coffee cups. It was the same almost every night: Grethe, beneath her bedcovers, would curl towards the bedside chair and listen as Berry spoke about things that were desperate and small. With the unfeeling city below, with its distant sirens and dots of electric light as ambience, they would be left alone, to say or not say whatever they pleased, until finally she would know nothing but sleep.

9

'I'm looking forward to the small-talk around the family table and to the dry bird that always gets stuck in my stepfather's throat... '

*

December.
The train pulled away from the station. Berry Walker looked over at Grethe; she was sitting in the opposite seat, with her suitcase between her legs. Her cheeks were red from the morning cold. She was wrapped in winter clothes, with a thick scarf pulled up to her nose.

Earlier, Berry had watched as Grethe had slept in his bed, her blonde hair spread across his pillows. She had rolled over and pressed him against the cold wall, but he had not minded. He had pulled the bedcovers tighter and listened to the sound of the birds outside. The light in his room had looked brown; it was the way the sunshine passed through the old floral curtains. He had known it was time for them to get up and leave. Only, Berry had wanted anything but to leave. For a moment, he had thought about not waking her, about keeping her captive in his bed, about ensuring that her plans went unfulfilled.

'So, you still haven't explained,' Berry started, leaning forward in his seat across the train carriage, 'why did you take so long to get ready in my room? You knew I was waiting for you downstairs… '

Soon, upon a metal bench and with an emptied polystyrene cup in his hand, Berry would be sitting alone. The airport would be filled with the echoes of rushed footsteps and dragged suitcases. He would be watching the sun rising higher, overpowering the humming lights of the lobby and illuminating the wet concrete outside. From the embrace they would have shared minutes earlier, he would still be feeling the sensation of Grethe's hair against his face. Of all the aeroplanes moving about below, he would not know inside of which Grethe would be sitting. At random, he would choose one to concentrate upon and as it rolled past, preparing to take flight, he would wave at it for longer than would be necessary, convincing himself that from behind one of the darkened windows, Grethe was waving back.

Berry added, to prompt her: 'so, what were you doing up there? You know, you nearly caused us to miss this train… '

Above her scarf, Grethe's eyes narrowed: she was smiling. The carriage was unusually quiet, but for the sound of the tracks below and the hushed voices of a few. Berry was suddenly conscious of his words being overheard, of there being others besides Grethe observing his failure to start a conversation. He refrained from asking her again. Instead, he leant back and from the newspaper that a businessman was reading beside him, stole an uninteresting paragraph. When he finally returned to Grethe, her muffled smile had disappeared and her face was blank. She looked as if she was in the grip of some puzzle or daydream, and so he no longer expected any response to arrive. She was an empty page, and so too would become the rest of the journey...

*

Later that day, Berry Walker was sitting in the room of his friend, Jack Fleeting. He was sipping some tea, staring at the walls and feeling tired. Whenever he was in Jack's room, Berry would always use a pile of magazines as a makeshift stool and sit there feeling as if the walls were staring back at him. For being fascinated with the groomed imagery inhabiting their pages, Jack collected fashionable magazines and covered his walls with pictures cut from them. The models they exhibited drew from him a strange adoration, not so much for their representations of high beauty and fashion, which they so forcibly prescribed, but rather for, as he claimed, the individual grace, form and tone of each. He liked to gaze back at them and admire shapes and shades and lines.

Berry felt glad that of the four rooms in his hallway, Jack's was only two along from his own. He had been someone easy to befriend. He was the archetypal, perpetual optimist, who wanted nothing but to play, to be under spinning lights, to be lost in the carefree. He was an advertiser's wet dream, for he consumed whatever he was told to, but he did so knowingly and this, in a sense, made him free.

'I hope I didn't disturb you before,' said Jack, his image being reflected in the mirror above the sink, 'only, I heard you come in early this morning and so presumed you were awake when I knocked...'

Whilst Berry sat there wearily, Jack was animated,

hovering around the sink and clawing the knots from his long hair with one hand. Jack complied with what most people consider to be a *normal* sleeping routine; he always got up early, irrespective of how little time he had spent beneath the quilt. His sleeping was consistent and required little effort to achieve. Berry Walker's sleeping habits, on the other hand, seemed broken beyond repair.

'I went with Grethe to the airport - she's gone home early for Christmas,' he replied. 'And no, I definitely wasn't asleep.'

Earlier, he had tried to sleep after returning from the airport, only to find his midday surroundings conspiring against it. There had been music from Jack's room two doors along; there had been footsteps thudding from the floor above; there had been car horns and sirens from the traffic outside; there had been images of Grethe whenever he closed his eyes. He had imagined that his bed, although it had long-since turned cold, was still warm from the night before, when he had shared it with Grethe. He had laid back and pretended that earlier, the alarm clock had never sounded and that she was still there. Then, prompted by the illusory warmth of the bed, he had become submerged beneath a waking dream, a dream he had pursued along an avenue into the past, before arriving at a time he had forgotten about until then. It had been a drunken memory from three months before…

Along a windowless black hallway, he was tripping over an invisible obstacle, losing his balance and having to lean against a wall. He was hearing noises from a party that was happening somewhere in the background; there were sounds of laughter and music littering the air. He was being led, absently drunk and without concentration, to a place he had never been before. He was squinting, trying to cut through the darkness, and seeing a white hat moving out of sight.

'Can you not be quicker, Berry Walker? Can you not find your way?'

He was pushing a door at the end of the hallway and entering a dark room. There were blankets hung up in place of missing curtains, with trickles of morning light coming through the small gaps between them. His eyes were adjusting to the darkness and he was able to distinguish the silhouette of a person in front of the windows. It was Grethe, definitely; she was standing beside a bed.

Next, he was moving cautiously towards her and then, once halfway across the room, feeling his feet getting tangled in a jacket left on the floor. Behind him, the door was swinging shut.

'Shhh!'

He was swallowing the reply he may have been about to say. He was lowering himself onto the edge of the bed and feeling relieved to be sitting.

'Shhh, Berry Walker! It's dangerous!'

The darkness was disorientating and the silence was dizzying. He was searching for a bedside lamp, hoping that it would end his confusion. He was finding one and turning it on.

'No! You should have stayed still. You should have stayed quiet… '

The light was strong and it was forcing him to rub his eyes. Through his parted fingers, he was finding Grethe; she was now over at the door, where she had rushed to when the light had come on. She was looking shocked.

Suddenly from behind him, there was a strict, male voice: 'WHO ARE YOU?'

Seconds later, having jumped away from the bed in reflex,

he was hitting the floor, hard. An unknown face was emerging from beneath the bedcovers.

'WHO ARE YOU?' the deep voice was repeating, 'WHO ARE YOU?'

He was scrambling back onto his feet, feeling drunk and confused. He was dashing toward the door, but in his haste, getting tangled again in the jacket and falling into the wall. He was sliding back down to the floor. He was looking up and seeing Grethe standing over him.

'Please stop, Berry,' she was saying, 'you don't understand… '

But he was no longer listening. He was getting up again and pushing her aside.

'Listen, this is not what you think… '

And then finally, he was swinging open the door.

'The man in my bed is my father!'

Once the daydream had subsided, Berry had sat up in his bed. His room had been filled with a familiar brownish light; the thin floral curtains were no match for the midday sun. He had given up trying to fall asleep. By then, his habit of overly-thinking about his need to sleep had sabotaged any chance of it happening anyway. To distract himself, he had reached over to his desk for a book to read, but could not find it. For some reason, the things that were usually there had all been re-arranged. But before he could investigate it further, there had been the sound of Jack Fleeting knocking upon his door…

2

I remember the first time I met Annelie Strandli.

I remember her coming into Jack Fleeting's room and sitting on the floor.

I remember her staring at the oddly decorated walls.

I remember her blonde hair running into the side of her mouth.

I remember Berry being quiet and pretending not to know her name.

I remember her stretching out her legs and tapping her shoes together.

I remember Berry leaving the room, to hide in the kitchen.

I remember her asking which pub we were going to that evening.

But more than anything else, I remember how different she appeared to how Berry Walker had described. For Berry had made it seem as if she was not beautiful.

*

Annelie Strandli was lazily spinning from side to side and listening:

'… telephones don't make you less lonely… '

From upon the high stool, she could see everything. The pub was large and plain. The few other people there were sitting mostly in pairs, discussing drink-laced things across small tables.

'… I just hate the distance between us… '

From the corner of her mouth, Grethe tried to blow her cigarette smoke sideways, away from her new friend.

'… and yet, for you, Grethe, the distance is even greater… '

Suddenly, the sound of familiar voices could be heard coming from the other room; they were cheering and clapping.

'… so please, tell me - how do *you* deal with it?'

Grethe placed her empty glass down and looked away: 'Well, I don't.'

Meanwhile, in the other room, I had taken the cue.

Meanwhile, in the other room, I had lined up the shot.

Meanwhile, in the other room, I had missed the ball and had already lost the game to Berry Walker.

With a smile that made him blush, Grethe thanked the barman, who had placed two more drinks upon the bar.

'Can I ask you something, Molly?' she turned back and said.

'Of course!'

Molly Colour was kind, unassuming and also very pretty, but subtly so, in a way that somehow befitted her name well. Some of her best qualities were ones of childhood – of earthy sweetness, of smiles for simple things, of concerning herself without prejudice to small matters of empathy – as if she had somehow managed to smuggle them, without losing their potency, into her emerging adulthood.

Grethe lifted one of the new glasses and sipped some wine from it: 'I'm thinking about another distant boy, but one who's distant in another sense. I first met him two nights ago, at a party on the seventh floor arranged by Jack Fleeting... '

The cheering from the other room had subsided. In its place, there was the sound of other people's conversations; the chatter of dressed-up boys and dressed-up girls was spilling over the edges of every table.

'Who?'

Grethe knew *his* name. Earlier, in the afternoon, she had approached a particular room on the seventh floor and met three people who had spun around to face her. Immediately, she had recognised *him* amongst them.

'... Berry Walker.'

Oddly, as she had approached that room, Grethe had heard her own name being mentioned inside. It had been said twice.

'What do you want to know about him?' Molly asked.
    'Anything.'

She had felt awkward standing in that doorway, and for not knowing what else to say, had simply repeated twice:
    '... did I just hear someone say my name?'

Molly delicately swirled the remaining wine in her glass: 'Well, I haven't known him for very long either... '
    'But don't you live on the same hallway as him?'

'Yes, in the fourth room, but I only moved in two days ago... '

It had become obvious that in the background, two clean-cut young men, wearing pressed shirts and with spiky hair, were trying to draw their attention. One of them winked and in return, Grethe shook her head.

Molly continued: 'However, I do know that he wants to be a writer... '

'Really? Who told you that?'

'Jamie Crook... '

'... did I just hear someone say my name?'

14

June.

Berry Walker was smiling with his eyes, and with them telling lies. He gazed the length of the table. The shadows cast by the hanging lights were making happy faces appear sinister. He was sitting at one end and hearing little of any sense:

'Olen ikävöinyt sinua, Annelie. Me kaikki olemme.'

'Minäkin olen ikävöinyt kotia. Ainakin sinun ruokaasi!'

'Oletko kuitenkin surullinen, kun jouduit lähtemään Lontoosta?'

'Kyllä, tietyllä tapaa olen hyvin surullinen. Se on niin mielenkiintoinen kaupunki.'

'Niin varmasti... '

The family scene was so carefree, so enjoyed by its participants, that the visitor was being easily forgotten. To seek some involvement, to feign some understanding, Berry nodded along and sank further into his seat. In his mind, which felt tired and irrational, the foreign words were concerned only with him, with his awkward presence, with the strange scenario into which he had entered, willingly.

'... me olemme kaikki iloisia, että päätit palata kotiin.'

'Eipä minulla tainnut olla paljon valinnan varaa... '

'Mutta mitä sinulle kuuluu, Annelie? Näytät hyvinvoivalta.'

'Kiitos, minulle kuuluu hyvää.'

The areas beyond the table were darkening: it was getting late. Berry turned to the window; the landscape outside was vast and quiet, and of the skyline there remained only the slightest hint of orange. He tried not to be preoccupied with the continuing conversation. He tried not to feel anxious. He tried not to dwell upon the fact that he knew not, with any real certainty, where he was.

'Me emme tainneet olla ainoat, jotka iloitsivat paluustasi, eikö niin Gunnar?'

'Totta. Sinähän tiedät, kuinka paljon toivoin, ettei meidän tarvitsisi olla enää erossa toisistamme, Grethe.'

'Tiedän... '

During momentary breaks in the dialogue, Berry could hear the sound of a loose windowpane softly rattling against its frame and submitted to this his full attention. In his stomach, he felt an enduring sensation of tightness, of apprehension, of exhaustion. He was trying to ignore the plate of food, colourful and plentiful to the point of almost overflowing, that he had left untouched upon the table.

'... mutta sain muutamia hyviä ystäviä Lontoossa ja nautin olostani siellä... '

'Niin.'

'... Oli vaikea lähteä.'

'Mutta, Grethe, eiväthän uudet ystäväsi ole koskaan olleet yhtä tärkeitä kuin se, mitä meillä on yhdessä. Tulet lopulta huomaamaan, että olet tehnyt oikean päätöksen... '

'Asia selvä, Gunnar!'

The sun then disappeared completely. From a shadowy region of the room, the family's dog, its eyes illuminated with Berry Walker's tired image, bared its teeth and made a growling sound only the visitor could hear. He felt like he was playing an extra in a scene he had been wrongly cast in. He knew that no matter how much he wanted to, he could not leave. Instead, he sank even deeper into his seat and allowed his mind to return to a time before his errors had been made.

… He closed his eyes and revisited the night before the trip, when he, unable to sleep and unwilling to vent his anxieties at his bedroom ceiling any longer, had gone to see his friend, Logan Waters…

'Oh.'

… He closed his eyes and was surrounded by smoke and wet canvases, by fumes rising from open paint tins, by the sound of his friend asleep in the next chair…

'Oh, I am so sorry.'

He opened his eyes again: someone was talking to him.

'I'm afraid that we all got a little carried away there… '

It was Grethe's mother: she had realised that once again, her family were neglecting to speak in English. Berry sat up in his seat. For a moment, he had forgotten where he was and had almost, but not quite, fallen asleep. With some effort he resisted the urge to yawn, causing his jaw to shudder instead.

'Really, Mrs. Strandli,' he cleared his throat to say, 'it does not bother me.'

Berry looked to the opposite end of the table, where Grethe was sitting. He tried to catch her eye, only to find her more concerned with her absent boyfriend, Gunnar, the boy whom it felt he had been acting the proxy for in London. Grethe looked happy; her cheeks were pink and her eyes were bright. She was eating her mother's food as if she had not eaten in weeks and tightly squeezing Gunnar's arm every time she laughed. Berry looked down at his plate and found that, much to his dismay, it remained as full as when he had left it to briefly daydream. He lifted his fork and despite feeling increasingly unwell, continued to eat, eager to show some gratitude toward his hosts.

'You know, Berry,' continued Mrs. Strandli, her spoken English sounding almost as perfect as her daughter's, 'Annelie has often talked about you… '

Berry did not know how to reply. Instead, his eyes were drawn back to Grethe; something in the whispered conversation she was having with Gunnar had made her laugh. She was covering her mouth with her hand, in case the food she was chewing escaped from it. After that, Berry was unable to return to his meal, to turn away from Grethe; she had come to hold, he realised, almost complete control over his will.

He recalled how he had simply followed her earlier, as if automatically, from the warmth of Logan Waters' room to the relative coldness of the family dinner. For fading alcohol, a growing fatigue and a profound inability to question the one who was leading him, he had made the journey as if he were under a spell. It was a trip that he now desperately regretted.

'Well, I speak about Annelie just as often,' he responded, finally. 'I can assure you of that much.'

Mrs. Strandli, who had been cupping her chin with the palm of her hand and waiting patiently for his reply, was looking back at him, curiously.

'My only hope,' he added, almost involuntarily, for having noticed Grethe receiving a kiss upon her swollen cheek and then feeling inexplicably candid, 'is that she feels as fondly about me as I do about her.'

He regretted those words before he had even finished saying them. He felt vulnerable, as if the room had inverted, and thought, but probably only imagined, that Gunnar had sent him a hostile look. The dog, which had been prowling for some time beneath the table, began to brush against his legs, as if it were taunting him.

'I… I mean,' he began to elaborate, hoping to shroud what he may have just revealed, to render forgotten any admission that he was, above all else – and quite irreversibly by now – in love with Grethe, only to mumble instead: 'I… I mean by that, of course… '

But luckily, he was interrupted, was left hanging over the precipice of the next word by Grethe's younger brother, who had reached for something across the table, prompting an outburst from his father:

'*Hei! Älä kurottele tuolla tavalla pöydän yli - pyydä ensi kerralla ojentamaan kulho, onko selvä?*'

'*Anteeksi!*' the boy blushed and retracted his hand, before turning to his mother to remark: '*Äiti, tämä on muuten todella hyvää.*'

'*Kiitos…* '

Once again, the talk amongst the table descended into words that were unintelligible to Berry, but he did not mind. The dog vacated the space around his feet and returned to one of the dark areas the hanging lights were unable to reach. Feeling grateful to have been spared from the discussion with Grethe's mother, he swallowed the awkward words he had been about to say. He then realised that his hands were shaking, causing his fork to clatter against his china plate. Wishing not to attract any attention from the others, he clamped his hands tightly between his thighs and exhaled a long breath. He tried to relax. The conversation, which had now grown to envelope the whole family, was as indecipherable as the language of the rattling windowpane he had earlier befriended, but he did not care.

'*No, Annelie, mitä suunnitelmia sinulla ja Berryllä on loppuviikoksi?*'

'*En ole vielä päättänyt mitään. Riippuu myös Gunnarista...*'

'*Gunnar, oletteko te kaksi tavanneet aikaisemmin?*'

'*Ketkä? Berry ja mina? Emme...*'

Berry had recognised his own name being mentioned and looked to its source: Gunnar. As he had dreaded, Gunnar's arrival at the house that afternoon had followed closely his own. He did not look the same as he had in the photographs on the wall above Grethe's bed; he was far larger and more handsome in real life. Berry watched him from the other end of the table. He looked at ease: his arm was wrapped around Grethe's shoulders and his attention was fixed upon the discussion. Whenever he spoke, tiny particles of chewed meat were flying from his mouth and settling on the table and on the clothes of the others. There were shadows across his face, making it difficult for Berry to gauge whether or not he was frowning.

'*... mutta olen kuullut hänestä paljon!*'

As the foreign words continued in the background, Berry started to feel another wave of exhaustion washing over him. It reminded him of how scarcely, if at all, he had slept the night before. Then, since it seemed that nobody was paying much attention to him anyway, he allowed himself to enjoy another moment of escape...

'*Niin, sanoin juuri Berrylle, että Annelie on puhunut hänestä usein.*'

... He closed his eyes and was staring at the clock in Logan Waters' room, was kicking the ground beneath his feet, was wishing that the morning would never arrive.

'*Toivon, että olet kertonut hänelle minusta yhtä paljon, Grethe!*'

'Totta kai olen!'

… He closed his eyes and was explaining how much he had feared losing Grethe.

… He closed his eyes and was describing how things had gone so wrong.

… He closed his eyes and was realising that his friend had fallen asleep.

… He closed his eyes and was wishing for the rest of this chapter to go missing…

10

In the mirror before which she was standing, Annelie Strandli caught a glimpse of the wooden desk beneath the windows. She tried to ignore the possibility of there being new pages hidden inside for her to find.

It's a story. It's a story without a name...

She had paused to observe her own image in the glass – her lips white with toothpaste, a brush hanging between them – and to fondly recall a conversation from a couple of weeks before:

... Everything went as we planned it, Jamie. His door was left unlocked. I looked inside his desk. You were right...

There were impatient sounds in the room. Reluctantly, she withdrew from the mirror and turned to find Berry Walker; he was lingering near the door, holding the handle of her packed suitcase firmly in one hand. He looked anxious: it was time for them to leave.

'I'll take this downstairs and wait for you there,' he finally said, 'but hurry, Grethe, or we'll miss the train and then your flight.'

Moments later, Grethe would be listening carefully to

the sound of Berry walking away. She would be holding her breath. She would be waiting for the echo of the stairwell door along the hallway. She would be anticipating her chance to move swiftly across the room.

'It's nearly Christmas,' she commented, watching him leave. 'Are you looking forward to it?'

*

Two

Reality was scarcely exciting and seldom free. Reality was a set of names written in chalk.

'It will be the same as yesterday,' said his friend. 'Only, please try not to fall asleep today... '

Boy One shrugged off his friend's advice and turned back around to face the front. Normally, he would seize every opportunity that arose to have a quick dream (and the classroom was always a fruitful arena in which for doing so), but today was different; today he felt conscious of being watched.

At the front of the classroom, Mr Letters picked up the register and, in strict monotone, began firing names into the air.

'... Yes!' Boy One called out at the appropriate moment, 'I am here.'

Boy One was a dreamer, a self-appointed professional no less, and professional dreamers never consider themselves to be 'dreaming too much'. Those of more regimented lifestyles, of orderly protocol, such as Mr Letters (who was a particularly out-spoken pro-reality activist), abide by the notion that through a simple examination of a person's progress in life, it can be determined whether or not they are a 'dreamer'. For example, Boy One's slumping school grades and limited ambitions were indicative that he was 'dreaming too much.' To such people, as their understanding of logic dictates, 'success' and 'dreams' were to be treated as opposing forces, as binary oppositions. Conversely, Boy One believed that some people did not dream enough.

... He suddenly realised that he was alone. There was nobody else around; the room was filled only with empty chairs. There was no writing on the blackboard any more, only a large smear of chalk in place of where the names of all the businessmen had been. There was silence everywhere and emptiness. But wait! - He began feeling something on his back... it was the feeling of being poked at... being poked at... being poked at...

'Will... you... ' Boy Two was saying, his finger jabbing in perfect harmony with his words, '... come... on... '

Boy One swung around, looked up and sighed: 'Oh, no.'

Together they walked out into the hallway, where busy people were streaming past. From a nearby drinking fountain, Boy One splashed some water onto his face.

'But how could I have known?' Boy Two explained. 'I was sitting behind you! You looked quite normal from where I was!'

'Oh no,' Boy One groaned again, as the water ran down his cheeks. 'Do you think anyone noticed me this time?'

'Well... '

'At least I can be sure that Mr Letters didn't see me,' he reassured himself. 'Surely he would have shouted at me if he had.'

They walked on.

'Well, let's just say that when the class ended, it was obvious you were asleep,' explained Boy Two, 'and everyone laughed at you.'

Boy One was not surprised. For having led such an extensive and prolific dreaming career, he was all too aware of how vulnerable he was during his bouts of internal meandering. He knew that his classroom escapism never went without consequence. His peers would ridicule him, would laugh and stare at his glazed expression and ill attention as he slumped in his seat, drifting somewhere beyond the room.

'What were you dreaming about anyway? I hope it was worth it.'

'Ah, nothing in particular.'

As they approached the canteen, the smell of food came rushing toward them.

'That's always the same for me too,' Boy Two commented. 'My dreams are never about anything in particular. It's a problem I have... '

'How do you mean?'

'Well, I rarely remember my dreams, but whenever I do, everything appears all jumbled up, all mixed up. If anything, all I can ever remember are just a few pictures... '

'You mean just photographs instead of film?'

'Perhaps,' Boy Two replied, 'but what I'm trying to say is that my dreams are always like drunken picture shows, over which I have absolutely no control.'

Entering the canteen, they each grabbed a plate and received some food. It was chips and baked beans, with lots of vinegar.

Boy Two continued: 'Now, some people say you dream about the last thing you were thinking about before you fell asleep, but I'm not so sure. I don't think it's that simple. For *example, last night I dreamt of a cat riding a bicycle... '*

'A cat riding a bicycle?'

'Yeah... but I certainly wasn't thinking hard about cats riding bicycles – or cats operating any machine for that matter – when I went to bed.'

They found two empty seats and sat down. Boy One looked down at his plate: the beans were of that thick, brilliantly orange consistency that can only be achieved by excessive simmering.

Boy Two quipped: 'I guess the next thing you're going to ask is whether or not I dreamt it in colour... '

'Well, did you?'

'Well, I couldn't tell... '

'Why not?'

'... because it was a black cat!'

Boy One laughed: 'But aren't black cats supposed to be unlucky?'

'Not this one!' his friend replied, smirking through a mouthful of soggy beans. 'Trust me, this cat put on one hell of a show!'

Boy One plunged his fork into his pile of chips, trying to spear as many as he could in one go. But then he noticed that the buzz of the canteen, together with his friend's laughter, had suddenly stopped.

Then, from behind, a hand grasped his shoulder.

'So, here you are,' began the hand, in deep monotone. 'I believe we have a meeting with one another at the end of the day... '

Sinking, and with a chill spreading across his chest, Boy One turned in his chair: 'We... we do, Sir?'

'Oh yes, we do, boy... '

Three

At the appointed time, Boy One timidly knocked upon the office door. The cold feeling of Mr Letters' hand grasping his shoulder had proven difficult to shake and all afternoon, wide-eyed with trepidation, he had thought about little else.

Momentarily, the secretary opened the door and guided him in. Mr Letters was sitting at his large desk, surrounded by piles of paper and stained polystyrene coffee cups.

'So, what am I going to do about you?' began the teacher.

Perching forward on his black leather chair, Mr Letters stared across the desk. Unable to return his glare, Boy One looked towards the secretary instead, who was sitting at a smaller desk to the side. She was busy chewing a pencil and picking dirt from underneath her long fingernails.

In the ensuing silence, Boy One was unsure whether or not his teacher was waiting for him to reply.

'Um... ' he eventually muttered.

'That was not a question.'

'Oh.'

'I do not understand you, boy,' started Mr Letters. 'Are my lessons really so boring as to warrant you falling asleep?'

Boy One did not answer.

'In nearly all of my recent lessons, you have fallen asleep, have you not?'

As he nervously maintained his focus upon the pencil that was being chewed to his side, Boy One felt a wave of red heat spreading across his face.

'Look at me!' Mr Letters blasted abruptly, bringing his fist down upon the desk and forcing his student to turn. 'What a waste of time you are!'

For not knowing what else to do, Boy One simply nodded.

'What do you think happens to people who sleep their way through my classes? I'll tell you what happens, boy - their name doesn't end up on my blackboard in twenty years' time...'

In the corner of his eye, Boy One thought he could see the secretary laughing, the pencil still hanging from her lips. His face began to itch with heat. He wished that Boy Two had been there to hear a line of Letters' so asinine.

'Do you seriously think that all of the successful, powerful people in the world spent their lives dreaming, just drifting along unconsciously?'

'No, Sir,' Boy One answered, rather feebly.

Mr Letters' glasses had become clouded. He removed them for a moment and released a frustrated sigh, before wiping them on the breast pocket of his shirt.

'Listen,' he added, his voice all of sudden showing some apparent sincerity, 'we make our own futures. Just remember that.'

'Yes, Sir.'

'Good. Now get out.'

Boy One, his face remaining awkwardly red, hovered silently towards the door and then pulled it open. But just as he was about to step outside, an arm reached over him and slammed the door shut again; for suddenly feeling an impulse to do so, Mr Letters had risen from his desk, stepped sideways along the wall and hurriedly blocked his student's escape.

'Actually, no... hang on,' he said, sternly. 'I am not finished with you, after all...'

That night, Boy One would be unable to sleep. He would lie awake in his bed, wishing he could erase his teacher's words from his memory. There would be so many things to think about that he would feel overwhelmed. It would seem as if his thoughts were all jostling for prominence; each one would seem frantic, hurried and be overlapped by another before it could reach its reasoned end. No structure or order of thought would be apparent and no progress would be made. He would stare up at his bedroom ceiling, the black picture through which he usually drifted to begin his dreams, only to see poisonous, repetitive words instead.

'... *I cannot help but wonder, what possesses a young man like you to be so very foolish?*'

Boy One stood still, receiving from his teacher a curious stare. He said nothing. From somewhere deep within his chest, he began to feel a sensation of tightness sweeping through his ribcage.

'Why do you persist in throwing away your life in sleep, in dreams? Do you not know how very dangerous it is?'

Mr Letters was looking down at him, with his head tilted and his eyebrows raised above his glasses, as if he were expecting an answer. But still, Boy One was incapable of saying anything.

'Let me tell you something, boy. Let me tell you something about sleeping too much... '

Boy One tried to breathe slowly.

'... Sleep is just a prelude,' the teacher explained, still holding the door closed with one hand. 'Sleep is just a prelude to death. The act of sleep, you must understand, is in itself a half-death, a dress rehearsal for the big black. Sleep is a fall into unconsciousness and death is only ever a matter of falling too far... '

In between every few words, Mr Letters was licking his lips and moving his free hand in various ways that empowered his *delivery.*

'… Let me ask you something, boy,' he continued, only now in a slower, more subdued manner that sounded quite sinister. 'Have you ever dreamt that you were falling from a cliff? Or that you were being chased by someone or something?'

The feeling of tightness in Boy One's chest was getting worse; it was morphing into a prickly heat and preventing him from speaking, even though he had absolutely nothing to say. He only wished that he was elsewhere, anywhere, and freed from the grip of his teacher's words.

'… Yes, boy, of course you have. We all have such dreams from time to time. Now, I ask of you this - have you ever hit the ground? Has your pursuer ever caught up with you? Yes, I am sure this has happened. We have all experienced such moments. But tell me, what happens when you hit the ground? What happens when the monster finally captures you? That's right - you wake up!'

Long strands of sweat were now reaching down the teacher's face. Having gradually leant forward, he had edged closer and closer to his student, until eventually his voice had needed only to be a whisper.

'And thus, we see the importance of waking up!' he proceeded to explain. 'Waking up is a mode of defence. One relies upon it to happen when one most needs it to - at that precise moment of impact, at that precise moment of capture. And it does always happen, now doesn't it? Well, it will only fail to do so once, and when that time comes, boy, it will be the end…'

Boy One felt a large lump in his throat and smelt the sickly-sweet aroma of sweat in his nostrils. He began nodding along in agreement, hoping that by doing so he might be released sooner.

'... *You must understand, boy, that in dreams one can never die, because one always wakes up just before the moment of death. But because of this, one never gets to see what happens after one has died. You see – and this is the crucial point – it is when one continues dreaming after one's own death, when one finds oneself staring down at his own body from on top of the cliff from which he has just plunged, that one has fallen too far.'*

Mr Letters paused for a moment and exhaled a long breath that brushed against his student's face, before continuing: 'and why is this, you may well ask? Well, it's simple really - because it's inhuman to see such a thing. One may never see oneself from outside of one's own body, except perhaps, after death. Alas, boy, it is a consequence of the human condition - one may never truly view oneself in the third person.'

The teacher leant back against the closed door. A line of sweat that had started at his brow finally slid into the side of his mouth. In the far corner of his eye, Boy One caught sight of the secretary again; she was staring at him with her mouth agape, the chewed pencil lying wet upon her lap.

Mr Letters rubbed his hands together, licked his lips and pushed himself away from the door. The secretary then scuttled over and opened it.

'Now, boy, be gone, but heed my words... '

Boy One said nothing. He moved slowly toward the exit, feeling relieved that his ordeal was finally over.

'... Do not go so idly into your slumber... '

He walked into the deserted hallway, his legs feeling unsteady.

'... or else suffer the fate of those who refuse to stay awake!'

Grethe exhaled. She imagined the bed, although it had long-since turned cold, was still warm from the night before, when she had shared it with Berry Walker. She lay back and pretended that earlier, the alarm had never sounded and that he was still there. The desk, which only by chance it seemed, had been left unlocked that morning, remained wide open. Grethe glanced at it and then, despite the time of her flight home for Christmas fast approaching, did little to resist the temptation posed by the unmade bed, to cast aside the clock and to daydream for a while. With the pages in her hand, she gazed into the future and was left enlivened by the view. She smiled, for knowing that in a place unseen by others, a place in darkness and in ash, there was the chance to uncover the secret writer, piece by piece.

Grethe was aware that Berry was waiting downstairs with her suitcase. She knew that by her absence he would soon be drawn back up to the room. She knew that she had to move immediately, or risk being caught in the act of secretly reading - only, she did not. Instead, she slowed her breathing until the pages, now resting upon her chest, scarcely continued to rise and sink, and felt the danger ebbing away. She was without worry. Soon enough, she would return the pages to their hiding place inside the desk and replace the items on top, even though, in her haste, she had failed to take notice of how they had been arranged before. Soon enough, she would climb into an aeroplane and, of all the glass buildings surrounding the runway, not know inside of which Berry would be waiting. Soon enough, she would be waving at a building chosen at random, convincing herself that from behind one of its large darkened windows, she could see Berry waving back.

6

I asked him to start at the beginning…

Berry Walker was swaying beside his bed, having just arrived back from a morning in the city. He dropped the bag he was carrying and then rubbed the aching spot on his shoulder where its strap had been. He felt tired. That morning, Jack Fleeting, eager for them to go record shopping together, had woken him up far earlier than he had expected.

… I asked him to tell me everything.

The November wind had blown Berry's hair in awkward directions, and now it kept wandering into his eyes. At the sink in the corner, he cupped his hands together and filled them with warm water to drink. In his room, the cold tap always ran slightly warm. But he always drank it anyway.

'But, Jamie,' he started, 'I don't know how to begin… '

I had brought with me a large bottle of alcohol. I used it to fill two glasses to the brim and then placed it on top of his wooden desk.

… It was Grethe's photographs; it was what they showed; it was how they reached him; it was how helplessly he returned their gaze:

Four legs intertwined in the sand… People healthy, and alive, and loved, in the summertime… Skin… Static eyes… A watchful arm wrapped around the shoulders of another.

… It was her telephone; it was the way the bells had teeth. *Ring Ring!* It was how she smiled against the shape of the plastic. *Hello, Goodbye.* It was how her conversations made no sense. *Ring Ring!…* It was the way it caused his city to implode.

'His name is Gunnar, by the way,' he explained. 'I know that now. I've found that out by myself. How? By her thoughts and by her memories - I read them all in her sketchbook. Did she really think I wouldn't skip back a few pages? No, of course not. She wanted me to and I couldn't help it… his name is written everywhere… and now I'm trapped… '

… It was the way in which the flashing light of the tallest glass tower came through her windows at night. And it was the way in which he could not stop it.

… It was the way in which Christmas would soon pull her away. And it was the way in which that watchful arm would soon wrap again around her shoulders.

… It was the way in which things were left unsaid.

… It was the way in which he…

… It was…

I asked him why he felt the need to tell me all of this now.
He looked down at his shoes, one of which was still stained
with red wine from an accident two months ago.

'Because,' he replied, 'I've just been writing something…
something without any meaning. That's not to say that Grethe
won't search beneath every word for some nonetheless… '

*

There was sound and there was light on the fifth floor, streaming
into and invading the hallway through Logan Waters' open
door. He waved at Berry Walker, having seen him passing by.
For always needing the company of others, the remedy to that
which he feared most – being alone – Logan Waters always
kept his door wide open. He studied Fine Art and so littered
his room with dripping canvases, with open paint tins, with
works in progress. He was a self-saboteur, whose internal life
was a party without noise or lights. Prescribing to himself
certain medicines that made the spaces beyond it easier to
neglect, he stayed mostly upon his bed and unconcerned with
the surrounding tides. He was happy to spend whole days
doing nothing but lying back and ambling about mazes of his
own making. He and Berry Walker had become good friends;
most nights, after Berry had left Grethe asleep in her bed, they
would drink away the silent hours, kneeling together before
the altar of Television.

When he reached Grethe's room at the end of the hallway,
Berry pulled her sketchbook from the bag he was carrying.
He had been loaned the sketchbook the day before and for
a moment, as he stood in front of her door, he stopped to
flick through its pages once more. He had reluctantly made
a contribution to it; a page that was messy and had been

hurriedly written, which he did not wish to read through again. He closed the sketchbook, readied his face with a smile and raised his fist.

But then, just before he could knock upon the door, he heard from the other side the sound of Grethe's voice. He leaned closer and listened: she was speaking to someone, in her native language, on the telephone.

And he pictured how happily her tongue was flapping...

And he pictured how loudly her heart was beating...

7

TEN EASY STEPS TO CONSCIOUSNESS

These buildings were built by the dead. And the stirring clerks I can see hitting keys inside, are also dead.

There are people walking along cracked concrete, toward lonely wine bars near Russell Square.

There are women selling flowers outside a church, just past Charles Dickens' old room in Tavistock Square.

More offices now.

"I LOVE IT WHEN THEY SCREAM MY NAME BECAUSE IT REMINDS ME WHO I AM"

Upon corporate steps the homeless are sitting frozen and drunk.

Discarded sandwich crusts. Empty plastic cups. The city is gripped by the frenzy of lunchtime. And a coffee shop window is saying: "Come in... Relax in one of our three floors..."

LONDON BOMB THREAT, NEW AND IMPROVED

I don't really know what you want me to say. I know you're expecting something more than this, and I am sorry.

ELDERLY AT RISK OF DYING YOUNG

... This newspaper served no purpose, but to be caught now in a draught from the window and blown around the seats.

WELCOME TO HOLBORN

A woman is lazing in a rooftop garden. She is feeling welcomed in Holborn.

A boy is pointing his camera at some pigeons. He is feeling welcomed in Holborn.

A preacher, holding above his head a cardboard sign, has a face like a man on the edge of a sword:

THERE IS NO MEANING LEFT BUT HIM

At the traffic lights there are cars waiting impatiently. The drivers want to be home, to be holding a cup of milky tea, to be in front of a narcissistic television-set that whispers, seductively: "Look at me, you're safe here... I'll show you things you've seen before..."

LOW HANGING TREES BEWARE

So, is there anything else to see?

Yes:

A cyclist wearing a gas mask. A girl, laughing. A hat lost in the wind. A businessman hugging his briefcase too tightly. An emptied package left abandoned upon a bench. A man averting his gaze from vomit spilt across the pavement. The two people behind me arguing about clothes. My reflection in the glass whenever we pass through a shadow. And the fascination that Jack Fleeting has with the lights of the shop windows passing by:

TODAY YOUR LAST CHANCE ENDS TODAY

I won't be much longer now.
I'm just crossing over Waterloo Bridge.
I'll step off in a minute.
And then I'll be there, Grethe... I'll be holding this... I'll be seeing you...

*

Lying in the dark, Annelie Strandli rolled over and stared at the silhouette of the bedside chair. Only shortly after having fallen asleep, she had woken up again, feeling alone. In her nocturnal room, everything was as it should be, except for the absence of Berry Walker. He rarely stayed for the entire night; typically, she would close her eyes and before they next opened, he would be gone.

Grethe always imagined that Berry would hurry away from

her room as soon as she had fallen asleep. She believed that rather than lying awake by her side, he preferred to spend each night at his old wooden desk. She often pictured him sitting up there, scrawling all that he wished to express and pursuing secret designs, designs that were perhaps concerned with her.

Grethe always kept a sketchbook by her bedside; it was mostly filled with her drawings, but also with her thoughts and memories. She turned on the lamp, wanting to check that Berry, as promised, had taken it with him. Earlier that evening, in grey lines and coloured patches, she had drawn a portrait of him in the sketchbook, depicting him wrapped in an itchy blanket and peering over some complicated book. In exchange for doing this, she had convinced Berry to fill the next page of it with whatever he pleased. It would prove to have been a most excellent trap, for the next day she would find the sketchbook returned and inside of it a page newly decorated with words.

Grethe smiled: upon the bedside table, there was an empty space where she had wanted one to be. She turned off the light and returned to sleep, unaware that the following afternoon, the new page – messy, partly illegible and consisting of fractured lines that veered up and down – would leave her disappointed.

*

The next day, I would be hiding from the afternoon sunshine beneath a pillow, when I would hear a knock upon my door.

'I hope this is not a bad time… but Jamie, can we talk?'

My visitor would be passing, rather anxiously, a single sheet of paper between her hands. And I would ask her to start at the beginning... I would ask her to tell me everything...

'Well, this morning Berry went into the city with Jack. And he took my sketchbook with him... '

*

"TEN... EASY... STEPS... TO... CONSCIOUSNESS... "

Grethe typed loudly on her childhood typewriter. She was busy translating word for word and onto a single sheet, the page that Berry had written in her sketchbook. Once she had finished she felt pleased; the words, which before had been difficult to read, were now in orderly rows that she could examine with ease. She pulled the sheet from the typewriter, folded it twice over and left her room.

In the hallway, drawn by the voices she could hear from inside, Grethe stopped at the doorway to Logan Waters' room.

'No, I'm sorry... I can't stay... I'm sorry,' she lied, somewhat shakily, declining Logan's request for her to come in and sit down. 'I'm actually just on my way upstairs, to visit Molly... '

Toward Berry Walker, who was slumped in a chair at the other side of the room, Grethe tried to silently convey her pleasure at having had her sketchbook returned so soon. An hour earlier, after finishing a telephone conversation with her mother, she had found it lying on the floor outside of her room. She wondered why he had left it there, rather than handing it back in person.

Then, feigning the appearance of being in a hurry, but not before asking Berry where he had gone that morning,

Grethe retreated from Logan's doorway. Once in the stairwell, she stopped to unfold and review her typed version of the sketchbook page again. The page remained disappointing, regardless of whether it was scribbled by hand or typed. After having pressed him for so long into writing something for her, she had received less than she had hoped she would. Little trace of herself, or her influence was apparent in the text. The page struck her as rushed, as written without much thought, and done simply to appease her, on a bus journey that morning between Camden Town and Waterloo.

*

'… If there is any meaning in this page, then I cannot see it. Either way, I shouldn't have to look so hard.'

I said there was something I wanted to tell her.

Grethe was sitting in the corner chair and drawing the last remnants of warmth from a cup of tea. 'You can trust me, Jamie. Whatever it is, I will not let Berry know that you've told me.'

Berry has been secretly writing something, I said. He told me so earlier today, when he came here to speak with me about something.

Grethe rose from her seat and, without realising she was doing so, slowly began to pace the room. 'He really said that to you? Do you think it's true?'

I nodded and watched as immediately, in her mind, fragments of a plan began to coalesce. To the perplexity of Berry Walker, and to the romantic dilemma that had been pulling her to and fro, she had seen a possible means of resolution, a means of viewing him as he truly was.

'Don't make me explain why I need this, Jamie, but I do. If any writings of Berry's actually exist, I have a suspicion about where their hiding place might be... '

Where? I asked.

'In his room, where the ashes from his cigarettes always land,' she replied fondly, with a smile. 'But first, I'll need to gain access to his room when he's not there. And for that, Jamie, I'm going to need your help... '

And when?

Impulsively, Grethe grabbed the typed page and, for considering it as having just been made redundant, as not offering the insight into the private world of Berry Walker she had hoped for, screwed it up tightly and cast it aside.

'Tomorrow,' she said happily, 'Let's allow ourselves to conspire for tomorrow... '

*

Tomorrow, for feeling unable to resist doing so, Annelie Strandli would ascend the stairwell with cautious footsteps. The hallway she would reach on the seventh floor would be dimly lit and grey. She would walk along it and from underneath each of the closed doors she passed by, feel rushes of cold air on her bare ankles that would make her shiver...

12

Berry Walker was sitting at his desk, sipping black coffee. He was anxiously waiting for the sound of Grethe's knuckles upon his door. The mist outside, which by the evening had thickened enough to obscure almost everything from view, was hugging the building and making his room feel small. At the large windows before which he was sitting, he found himself beginning to unwillingly stare. The glass was white like a blank page and he quickly became lost in it, thinking about the evening ahead.

At the restaurant where he was planning to take her, Berry was intending to confront Grethe about the near future and about why she would become flustered and evasive whenever the subject was raised. By the manner in which she had been using her telephone – by the tone of her words and by the traits of her tongue – he had gathered enough reason to become concerned. It was his suspicion that in the summertime, by an absent boyfriend whose pressuring had proven too difficult to resist, by foreign influences that Berry had little chance to undermine, Grethe had been persuaded to drop out of her studies and leave London for good. In fact, he was convinced of it. He fantasised that later at the restaurant, with her hand upon his and her blonde hair running into the side of her mouth, she would agree to not leave, to reverse her plans and stay with him instead.

*

Two months later, at the edge of her family home, in a room that would feel somehow familiar, Berry Walker would be lying with his head buried beneath Grethe's childhood bedcovers. The bed would be small and warm, a soft enclosure within which he would be trying to feel, if only for a moment, alone.

'I have prepared Annelie's old bedroom for you,' Grethe's mother would have said, having seen Berry's shivering limbs and blackening eyes at the dining table. 'Please go and use it, Berry, if you wish.'

But it would be hard to feel alone. Despite his retreat from the table, the house would remain alive and new discussions would be drifting underneath the door. In particular, Berry would be able to distinguish the sound of Gunnar's voice; he would be sounding more animated and far happier than before. Then, upon the black underside of the bedcovers, he would see a vision of Gunnar and Grethe, happy and safe and entangled in one another, in the basement bed it would have been arranged for them to share. The thought of them together would cause Berry to feel claustrophobic and uncomfortable, as if the air he was breathing had become thin and over-used.

He would push off the bedcovers and by exposure to the room, feel quickly revived. The clothes he would remain wearing, which he would not have had the energy to remove before, would be twisted and tight around his body. He would straighten them and look around, wondering about what artefacts of Grethe's he might find himself surrounded by. He would imagine there being dusty books, old letters, cassette tapes and school photographs all within his reach, but for then at least, he would want nothing but to sleep.

He would begin detailing a trip he might have taken through the bedside window – to be a companion to the moon, to be a part of the dark landscape, to be a frozen cadaver found weeks later in the valley – and would keep his mind busy until it was clouded with sleep. Finally, he would drift off, only to discover that a vision of Gunnar and Grethe, happy and safe and entangled in one another, would be the only subject he could dream about. And by this, he would finally succeed in feeling alone.

13

Annelie Strandli adored her photographs; it was what they showed; it was how they reached her; it was how helplessly she returned their gaze. Earlier, Catrina Bloodly, as she had been passing critically through Grethe's sketchbook, had unknowingly knocked some of them off the wall above the bed. Grethe picked up the photographs, which were lying face down upon the pillows, and then left her room.

Shortly, once on the seventh floor, she could smell something burning; in the shared kitchen at the end of the hallway, Jack Fleeting had put some food underneath the grill and then forgotten all about it. Grethe knocked upon Berry Walker's door. She looked down at her dress, which she had been looking forward to putting on all day, and brushed out any creases that remained in it.

'Grethe! What happened?' Berry asked her, after opening the door. 'What have you done?'

'Oh, you mean this?' she replied, holding up one hand, two fingers of which were temporarily wrapped in damp tissues. 'I had an accident involving a cigarette earlier. I wasn't paying attention… I was daydreaming about Home.'

Berry invited her in and as she walked over to the bed, Grethe's eyes were drawn immediately, and as if by their own accord, toward the wooden desk. She fantasised about how their evening together at the restaurant might transpire, about how after their meal, Berry might finally reveal his secret writings to her. She believed that it was for this reason that he had wanted to take her there.

'Home?' Berry replied, rather coldly, as he closed the door and followed her over. 'What caused you to think so deeply about that?'

Before she answered, Grethe lay down, causing the plastic around the mattress to crackle: 'I don't know... I suppose I just miss being there sometimes, that's all.'

Berry opened one of the misty windows, to dilute with fresh air the aroma of burnt food that had followed them into the room. A rush of coldness quickly forced Grethe beneath the bedcovers, kicking her shoes off over the edge of the bed.

'So, when are you next planning on going home anyway?' he asked.

'In the summertime, I think, perhaps in June. Speaking of which, Berry, I thought you might like to join me next time? It would be nice if you came and stayed with me there, if only for a week... '

Grethe looked at Berry; he was now sitting in the seat before his desk, lifting a mug of black coffee to his lips and sweeping away strands of dark hair from his eyes. He was looking back at her strangely, as if there was something on his mind that he dared not say, however much he wanted to.

'Hmm, I'm not sure about that,' he replied unsteadily, after a minute or two, 'although I do wonder, Grethe, how long are *you* planning on staying there this time?'

Grethe rolled over to face the wall, as if by doing so she

could be excused from answering the question, and closed her eyes. Thereafter, for some minutes, regardless of however much he prompted her to speak, she remained silent and still. She did not wish to answer; she did not wish to injure him.

*

Four

"At one end of the town, Boy One lay in his bed and swung at his alarm clock with a clenched fist. The sunlight behind his curtains was cold.

At the other end of the town, Mr Letters lay in his bed, clenching his legs around his bedcovers and curling up onto his side. The sunlight behind his curtains was warm.

The bronze bell above the door chimed.

'Oh, hello there... do you not have school today?'

'Yes, I do, but I don't feel much like going. I didn't sleep last night.'

That morning, Boy One had been running late when he had left his house. Reaching the edge of the park, he had spotted Boy Two in the distance; he had obviously grown tired of waiting for him at the corner where they usually met before school.

'Oh? And why didn't you sleep?'

'There's something on my mind,' he replied, moving toward the counter. 'Can I talk to you about it?'

'Of course.'

On the shelves behind the counter, the tall jars of sweets, of all different shapes and colours, drew his attention for a few seconds. The shop was empty. And so felt his body.

'I'm scared,' he began. '... I'm scared of dying in my sleep.'

Boy One still felt entangled in the echoes of his teacher's words and realised that for the first time ever, he had passed through an entire night without sleeping. Earlier, he had got up, had got dressed, had made some food and then thrown it away.

It seemed that Mr Letters had affected Boy One deeply. He had hung on the teacher's every word, as if what he had been hearing were concrete facts, as if he had been privy to a truth unknown to others.

'It all makes sense,' he had reasoned to himself. 'After all, why else would the process of going to sleep always be referred to as falling?'

Boy One ran hurriedly from the shop and into the park.

'Death?' Old Man had said. 'Death is chaos... '

He paced around on the grass for a few moments, chewing one of his knuckles until it was red.

'... and there is only one means of making order of chaos...'

Upon a nearby bench, beneath a bare tree, he finally sat down and covered his face with his hands.

'... and that is through an act of creation.'

Boy One had been in search of reassurance, of protection. He had seen his habit of idly dreaming whenever he pleased as being under threat. He had seen a risk left unrealised for too long, a risk hiding in the farthest corners of his sleep, a risk across which his wandering mind might stumble at any moment. And yet, Old Man, with his lips wetted and his eyes fixed, had leant forward over the counter and thrown forth wild, stabbing words of crazed beauty, to reassure and to protect him:

'You must create something, anything. Creating something,

however small, will make your future more secure. Trust me… '

Boy One felt wearier than he ever had before. It felt as if his eyes were sitting in dry sockets. It felt as if his brain was being squeezed like a wet sponge.

'… it will make less uncertain the future.'

And between his parted fingers, he blankly stared down at the dead leaves beneath his feet.

'… it will make less daunting the end.'

Five

That night, lying awake in his bed and muttering out loud to himself, Boy One pledged that his lifestyle, his sleeping career, would never be corrupted again. He needed a means of security, of defence, a means of evading the cliffs and of evading the pursuers, a means of making the threat of ever falling too far redundant.

He lay back and there were blueprints in the darkness:

'What if one could gain control over his dreams?'

… And there were blueprints in the darkness:

'What if Boy Two could gain the ability in his dreams to command his black cat?'

… And there were blueprints in the darkness:

'What if I could gain the ability in my dreams to… yes… '

It was not until the end of the night, as the sun was breaking, that Boy One felt the will to sleep, the ability to relax once more. High upon the ceiling, the canvas upon which notions collided and imagery unwound, he had seen the answer painted. After that, he no longer cared about the creeping light, or about the creeping time, for he had created something, something that could now be drawn whenever he closed his eyes, whenever he sank beneath his bedcovers, whenever he drifted beyond a day-

lit room. By no means other than the colourful logic of his own introspection, Boy One had created..."

'Wait!' Grethe would look up and say. 'Did you just hear that, Jamie?'

Having been startled by something, she would drop the interrupted pages, jump to her feet and quickly move across the room.

'It might be Berry! He might be back!'

She would place her ear flat against the back of the door. She would be frightened by the thought of approaching footsteps, envisaging how she would have left the desk next door – the lid flipped open, the things on top pushed aside, the inner compartment emptied – only to be relieved a few minutes later. Only then, when nothing further could be heard, would she return to the corner chair and to the unfinished story...

And I would watch again as her hands found the next page.

And I would watch again as her eyes found the next line.

And I would watch again as her mouth formed the next word:

"... She.

Later that morning, by the ringing of the bell above the shop door, Old Man was drawn from the small stockroom behind the counter, where he had been busy arranging sweets into different piles by their flavour, shape and sourness.

'I need to tell you something... '

Old Man brushed off the traces of coloured sugar that had gathered upon his shirt and trousers, before looking across the shop floor. His visitor, trailed by the brown leaves that had been swept in as he had hurried through the door, was approaching the counter with an eager look upon his face.

'I need to tell you something,' he repeated.

Old Man lifted himself up onto his high stool and frowned: 'What is it?'

'She.'

'What?'

'My resolution to all chaos!'

Old Man turned around and, over the stacked jars standing on display, peered out through the window and into the park. He saw a dog running after a ball thrown by its owner. He saw a boy and a girl sitting cross-legged upon the grass, sharing the fizzy shapes he had sold them minutes before. Then, for catching a skewed image of himself in the glass as he withdrew his focus, he paused momentarily for reflection and realised that he had neglected to mention something important. By his own act of creation, writing, he had been able to place his future and his past into relative context, to make sense of his own internal confusions, his own matters of chaos. However, in all of his long life, there had always been one subject that had remained unsettled, one perpetual trouble that he had never been able to resolve:

'Love,' he said, turning back. 'But what about Love?'

But Boy One had been paying little attention. He too, over the shop-front display, had been peering out through the window, but he had not been viewing the park, or the dog running after the ball thrown by its owner, or the boy and the girl sitting cross-legged upon the grass. Instead, he had been viewing the image of his creation, She, reflected back at him in the glass.

'Love?' he replied, without breaking his gaze from the imaginary spot upon which his eyes, growing wider and drier,

had become fixated. 'You're asking me about Love?'

He was suddenly interrupted by the bell above the shop door, by the slapping of leather shoes across the tiled floor, by the rustling of a paper bag being opened, by the thudding of coins being laid upon the counter, by the crunching of hard sweets between two sets of teeth.

Once the customers had left and silence had resumed, Boy One finally broke his stare. For a moment, the electric lights stung his eyes. He desperately needed to have everything explained, to have everything released into the atmosphere. He turned to his friend to begin and then, in remembrance of his darkened ceiling, the place where he had first glimpsed the means of gaining some control over his dreams, some protection against ever falling too far, he felt a smile spreading across his face. It was a smile the size of which he had never known.

'The only thing I know about Love,' he started, 'is that my creation is Love... '

Boy One felt as if he had always been in love with someone, only someone he had yet to meet, someone separated from him by distance and by time. His creation, which he had begun to refer to as She, was simply an imagined illustration of this unknown girl.

'... and with it, I will live each day... '

It was Boy One's intention to have the image of She become stained upon his sleeping mind. By careful self-conditioning, by concentrating his thoughts prior to going to sleep, he would ensure that She lay more heavily upon his subconscious – and therefore feature more frequently within his dreams – than any person he knew.

'... and with it, I will feel no danger... '

Thereafter, She would not only act as his companion within

*his dreams, but also as his guardian. She would be the reason
for which his premature death could be dismissed. By being a
representation of a future in which he very much believed, and
therefore providing the evidence that he had one, She would
prevent him from ever falling too far. She would be the hand
that grabs him at the edge of the cliff. She would be the foot
in the alleyway that his pursuer trips over. She would be the
alarm that delivers him to the surface at the moments he most
needs to be conscious.*

'... and with it, I will forever know when to wake up...'"

*

Come in, I said.

'Jamie, do you know where Berry has gone?' asked Grethe,
as she walked in and closed the door securely behind her. 'He
was supposed to take me out to a restaurant this evening, but
he's disappeared and now it's too late for us to go... '

Perhaps only an hour after having accidentally fallen asleep
in his bed, Grethe had woken up alone in Berry's room. She
considered how tired he must have grown of her silence, how
tired he must have grown of sitting there – his mug of black
coffee left to go cold, his dark hair left to cover his eyes, his
question left to dissolve into the air – before he had stopped
waiting for an answer and had left her alone.

'Well, it doesn't matter whether or not I know where he is,'
she continued, 'only, I hope there's enough time for what I've
brought you, Jamie...'

Once again, Grethe had found Berry's desk unlocked
and, much to her delight, that the pages inside were more
substantial than before. With her finger, she stroked an area

on the covering page that had been burnt by some discarded cigarette. She always wondered why it was that Berry Walker persisted to use that dangerous hole in the top corner of his desk.

'I want to share this with you, Jamie,' she said as she straightened her dress, which had become all tangled and folded during her brief sleep. 'I want you to understand what I've been coming to talk to you about for all this time... '

Grethe laid the pile of pages upon her lap. She explained how the story had been leaving her confused, how she had detected little tangible meaning, or relevance to her and Berry's situation in it so far.

My immediate suggestion was that she might be looking too hard.

Grethe sighed. For months she had been delving into the pages in search of subtext, of directions, of implicit signposts toward the writer's character, but without success. She had come to convince herself that unless she found some underlying meaning in it soon, she may as well have not read it at all.

'... I'm going to read it out loud to you now,' she said, looking down at the first page and wetting her lips, 'I'm going to read it out loud from the very beginning... '

And I watched as her hands found the first page...
   And I watched as her eyes found the first line...
   And I watched as her mouth formed the first word...

3

There were people from unknown hallways, dressed in colourful clothes and dancing with careless feet. Occasionally, a flash from a camera would light everything up and capture an image of a dance, a drunken tumble, or a group of people posing with their arms around one another.

Berry Walker was standing at the edge of the room, with a fresh drink in his hand. With forced interest, he was nodding along with a person who was passionately speaking to him about something he cared little for: Economics. As he continued to listen, or at least, give the impression that he was listening, he glanced beyond their shoulder and surveyed the party. The room was full. There were approximately one hundred people living in the building and most of them had answered Jack Fleeting's invitation to fill the lobby-area of the seventh floor. Berry observed the people dancing and noticed how it looked as if the colours of their clothes were chasing after them, always a split-second behind their twisting bodies.

Suddenly, there came a loud noise to the side of where Berry was standing. With a shudder, and far short of where it was supposed to, the elevator had stopped abruptly. There was a person inside; they could be heard frantically banging their fists against the metal door. Berry looked over and saw Jack hurrying across the room. As the spokesperson of his party, Jack had spent the evening trying to meet as many new people as possible and the person trapped in the elevator was to be no exception.

Berry went to help Jack and between them, they managed to prize open the door of the elevator and lift out the person from inside.

'Thank you,' the trapped girl said as she stepped out into the commotion, 'I was really starting to panic in there.'

'You're welcome,' Jack smiled, extending his hand and shaking it with hers. 'My name's Jack, by the way, and this is Berry Walker.'

'It's nice to meet you both, but what's going on here? I only moved into the building today.'

Darkness was creeping in through the windows, reducing the dancers to silhouettes and fuzzy shapes. No-one else, it seemed, had noticed the elevator being forcibly opened.

'Jack will explain everything,' answered Berry, 'whilst I go and get you a drink to calm your nerves... '

On the floor of the kitchen, there was a drunken girl dressed in white, slumping against one of the cupboards. She was refusing to stand, regardless of however much her friend, who was playing her attendant, tried to pull and persuade her to.

'Oh,' Berry Walker mumbled weakly, as he peered around the doorframe.

For most of the night, Berry had remained near the makeshift bar and drinking steadily. However, by then the bar had been emptied and so he had needed to venture elsewhere for another drink.

'… erm, don't mind me… '

With his eyes set upon the fridge and his mind upon the premise that a forgotten bottle or two might still be inside, Berry began to skirt around the edge of the small room. The girl laughed and then shouted something indistinguishable. It was the same thing he had heard moments earlier, as he had paced along the hallway toward the kitchen, carefully stepping over the bodies of half-conscious people as he went.

'Tulen Venäjältä! Ja vaadin saada drinkin!' the girl shouted.

Berry reached the fridge, believing that he had successfully avoided drawing too much attention from the girl, only to feel a hand grasp his ankle.

'Hey!' he stumbled and glanced down.

He turned back to the fridge, trying to keep his balance as the girl pulled at his leg. Much to his delight, he found a large bottle at the back of the shelf, one that had somehow been overlooked before.

'I'm from Russia!' the girl said again in a cracked voice, only this time in English. 'And I demand a drink!'

Berry smiled awkwardly at her and tried to shake his leg free from her grip.

'Damn it!' the girl's friend then yelled. 'She only moved in here earlier today - and now look at her!'

Berry tried to appear as if he cared, although all he really wanted to do was leave.

'Give me a hand, will you?' she continued. 'You grab her on this side, and I'll pull her up from the other… '

Meanwhile, in the other room, I found Jack Fleeting; he was standing shakily against a wall. As I approached him, he turned to the person beside him and started:

'Molly Colour… '

And I reached out my hand to greet her.

'… I want you to meet one of your new neighbours, Jamie Crook… '

The girl started to sway again. Before she could fall back, Berry quickly caught her underneath her arms. In a language he presumed was Russian, she began to talk at him again. He moved away from the fridge, fearful that with one of her flailing arms, she might knock the bottle he had left standing on top of it.

'Tulen Venäjältä! Ja vaadin saada drinkin!'

Berry looked at the girl and from beneath the white hat that had fallen down to cover much of her face, caught her smiling at him.

*

The following night, Berry Walker was lying awake in his bed and shaking a metaphysical fist at the sleep he had lost. It had been hiding somewhere, the promise of sleep, in places he had been unable to reach. Although he was exhausted, his mind was restless and loud; it had been contaminated with a drunken image of a particular girl. Under the weight of the previous night's excesses, he had spent the day thinking and talking about things in circles. He could remember every detail of every person he had met at the party, except for the person he most wanted to. Although he did not know the Russian girl, or particularly wished to – for her appearance at the party had not advertised her character well – his thoughts had kept returning to her nonetheless.

At the end of the party, when the air had become thick, when most people had already left in hope of desperate sleep before it grew too bright, Berry had seen her again. Dawn had been approaching through the grid-lined windows and he had been slouching in a plastic chair, with his last drink in his hand. By then, the only people who had remained had dispersed to the edges of the room, where there had been just enough shadows left to cover them. They had been sharing weary discussions, hunching over final drinks, or staring into the fading faces of others.

For a moment, Berry had closed his eyes and immediately felt someone snatch the dead cigarette left hanging from his lips.

'Thank you!'

When he had opened his eyes again, he had seen white clothes; they were marked with shades of grey from the kitchen floor. He had mumbled and rubbed his eyes.

'Thank you,' the voice had then repeated, 'that's something we say in the East... '

Berry had straightened his back against the cold wall: 'What - Thank you?'

'Yes.'

The girl had been slurring her words. As she had sat down on the floor beside him, Berry had leant back on his chair, far enough for it to feel as if its plastic legs might break, and drawn in a deep breath. He had pictured her from earlier that night and foreseen a drunken conversation in which he had felt unwilling to indulge.

'Why are you thanking me?' he had asked, coldly.

'For the cigarette, of course.'

Berry had said nothing. He had considered it strange how much she had changed in a matter of only two or three hours. She had lit the plundered cigarette, before loudly declaring that she was from Russia.

'Yes, you've already told me that,' he had sighed.

Berry had reached into his pocket, in search of more tobacco. He had felt her staring at him. For not knowing what else to say, he had looked elsewhere, anywhere, and in doing so had realised how bright everything had become. Clean light had begun to invade the building; it had been creeping down the walls the higher the sun had raised.

'Hmm... are you enjoying my hat?' she had said, pushing her white hat in a circular motion around her head.

Berry had looked over: she had been peering back at him, somehow endearingly, with one red eye.

'Well?' she had added.

With that, Berry had conceded a smile and passed to her the bottle. But she had spun it across the floor and into the middle of the room.

'There's nothing left,' she had frowned, stubbing out the cigarette upon his shoe.

Although his chances of finding anything else to drink had been slight, Berry had gone to look nonetheless. There had been nothing in kitchen, except for a smashed bottle of red wine, which he had stepped in, staining one of his shoes. With one wet foot, he had then headed back to the girl, but over sleeping legs in the hallway, had stumbled and fallen along the way.

Berry shook away his recollections and looked over at the clock beside his bed: *eight*, it said. The morning birds were breaching the closed windows and singing into the room. He was never happy to hear them; they were part of the ensemble that always surrounded his sleeplessness. He peered between the curtains and looked outside: the houses along the streets were crowded together like a jigsaw and the river was shining brightly yellow, as if it were a scene from a glossy postcard. He saw no use in lying there any longer. Instead, he decided to do something about the large pile of dirty clothes that had accumulated in the corner.

Shortly, as he was spiralling down the stairwell to the ground floor, where a small room with three old washing machines could be found, the coldness of the stone beneath his bare feet made him shiver. Once in the laundry room, he filled one of the machines with his dirty clothes, inserted a coin and listened as it started to whirr. Beneath the cracked window on the far side, he sat down on the floor and raised a book he had brought for company. Inside the spinning drum, to a mechanical rhythm that was almost hypnotic, the clothes began to dance. Within minutes, he felt not the energy, nor concentration to read the book and quickly found that his mind, set against the rotating soundtrack, was becoming careless and heavy…

The first thing Berry felt when he woke up was the sun; as he had slumped there asleep, it had risen high enough in the sky to shine through the window and warm his shoulders. The next thing he saw was his book; it was lying on the floor in a patch of sunshine, its cover accidentally folded under his shoe. It felt as if he had been asleep for only a few minutes, rather than for the remainder of the morning.

'Good afternoon,' a female voice said.

He looked up: a blurry person came quickly into focus, like the sharpening of a subject through a camera lens. It was someone he recognised.

'Well, that's a strange place to sleep,' she added.

'Sorry,' Berry mumbled, instinctively feeling as if there

was something he should apologise for.

'You know, I've been in here for a while, sorting through my washing… '

'Oh.'

'You're a quiet sleeper.'

As she emptied the contents of a large floral-patterned bag into the machine beside his, Berry slid up the wall and onto his feet, brushing the dust from his trousers.

'I remember you,' he said to her, 'I remember you from the party. Only, I never caught your name…'

*

I was sitting in Jack Fleeting's room, sipping some tea and flicking through one of his many magazines, when Berry Walker, having returned from downstairs, walked in with a knowing smile upon his face.

'Berry! Where have you been all morning?' asked Jack. 'Jamie and I were looking for you… '

Jack had been standing with his back to the door, wearing thick headphones and dancing to himself. Berry had entered the room and tapped him upon the shoulder to gain his attention.

'Why? What time is it?'

'It's two in the afternoon,' Jack replied. 'We wanted to ask if you fancy coming out with us this evening.'

'Where to?'

'Oh, just some pub I know, not far from here. I'm going to invite Molly too.'

'Who's Molly?'

Jack took off his headphones and moved to the middle of

the room, to stand with Berry and I: 'She's the girl from the party who was trapped in the elevator. Do you not know yet, Berry? She's living in the fourth room of our hallway, she moved in two days ago!'

Berry scratched his head and as he did so, glimpsed his own reflection in the mirror above Jack's sink. He looked exhausted: there were thin branches of red stretching across his eyes.

'Oh, right,' he responded, before changing the subject: 'but anyway, I need to tell you both about something...'

'Go on... '

'Well, I fell asleep in the laundry room this morning and when I woke up, I met someone... '

Catrina Bloodly was quite pale, with hair that was cut horizontally across her brow and draped long down the sides. She always acted as if there was a camera following her, a camera that captured her image to have it placed at the forefront of some fabricated show. During her and Berry's conversation in the laundry room, she had imagined the camera was hovering just outside the window behind Berry and capturing, through the cracked glass, a perfect over-the-shoulder shot of her performance. Berry had shaken her hand weakly, before starting to pull his wet clothes out from the machine. With an image of Catrina drawn from his memories of the party – of her in the kitchen, struggling so exhaustedly to control the Russian girl – Berry had opened a conversation and thereafter, had been told everything he had wanted to know.

'... and so, as it turns out, the Russian girl I told you about before isn't Russian, after all.'

'What do you mean?'

'She's Finnish, according to her neighbour, Catrina. She lives on the fifth floor.'

'Okay.'

'And her name is Annelie... Annelie Strandli,' Berry concluded, as if by saying her name twice out loud, it would become cemented to the image he held of its owner.

Then at that moment, there came an unexpected voice from the doorway:

'Hello? Did I just hear someone say my name?'

Berry spun around and as he faced the person smiling at him from the hallway, tried his hardest not to appear surprised.

'Did I just hear someone say my name?'

4

The spats of rain striking the windows looked like small lacerations on the glass. Over the top of the drink she had raised to her lips, Grethe peered across the table at Berry Walker. During their time sitting together, he had been drinking almost continuously and his cheeks, which were normally quite pale, had gradually become redder.

'So, I'm curious,' he asked, 'if your name is actually Annelie, then why are you known as Grethe?'

For reasons that now seemed absurd, Grethe had felt anxious about first approaching him in the pub that evening.

'But look - there he is now,' Molly Colour had said, having looked over and noticed that both Berry and Jack had entered from the other room. 'Perhaps, Grethe, you should go and find out about him for yourself… '

But Grethe had felt unsure. Everyone had been easy to meet, except for Berry Walker: earlier, he had been quiet; earlier, he had claimed not to know her name; earlier, he had left the room to hide in the kitchen.

'Go on,' Molly had nudged her, 'I'll get rid of Jack for you… '

When she had finally approached him, Berry had been sitting alone in a cloud of smoke, waiting for Jack to bring over some drinks from the bar. Looking bored, he had been occupying himself by reading the drinks menu on the table top, over and over.

'Well, my full name is Annelie Margrethe Strandli,' she answered. 'I guess that Grethe is just an obvious abbreviation of that...'

'But isn't Ann more obvious?'

'Hmm, good point, but apparently not,' she smiled. 'Only my parents call me Annelie.'

Looking beyond Berry's shoulder, Grethe noticed that she was still being stared at from afar. And her smile quickly faded.

'Can I buy you another drink?' asked Berry, as he slid his chair back and stood up.

But Grethe no longer felt at ease. The two tidy young men, who had made suggestions toward her and Molly earlier, were still sitting in the corner with their legs wide open and their eyebrows raised. One was tilting his head and beckoning to her with one finger.

'Actually, Berry,' she replied, 'I don't want to stay here any longer.'

'What's wrong?'

'Nothing... it's nothing.'

'But why?' he asked, passing his empty glass between his hands. 'It isn't closing time yet... '

'I know, but I no longer like this place very much.'

*

There were no shelves in Berry Walker's room, or decorations upon the walls, only piles of things organised by similarity, spread around the floor and furniture. That was the first thing Grethe noticed after being invited in. The second thing she noticed was the old wooden desk beneath the windows.

Outside the wind was cold and directionless, rushing between the houses and waving about the arms of the trees above the streets. As she and Berry had walked home together, leaving the pub far behind them, Grethe had bunched her damp hair together and wrapped it forward over her shoulder. Apart from the flashing light upon the tallest tower of the financial district, which had trespassed into the corner of her eye, the same as it did into her room each night, the park had been almost entirely dark. She had felt glad not to be walking through it alone.

Sitting on the edge of his bed, Grethe looked over at Berry; he was in the chair before his desk, rolling a cigarette.

'Did you meet a boy called Logan Waters at the party two nights ago?' she asked. 'He lives two rooms along from me.'

Berry shook his head and commented that the name *Logan Waters* sounded as if it belonged to a character in an American cop show from the 1970s.

Grethe laughed: 'No, he's a painter, actually. I'll introduce you to him sometime - I have a feeling you two will get along.'

She began nursing a small tear that her jacket had suffered during their walk back. After leaving the park, they had entered a narrow pathway beside the railway tracks, enclosed by rusted wire fences on either side. Momentarily, the turbulence from a passing train had rattled the fences and caused a strand of jagged wire to become caught in the upper arm of her jacket.

'Actually, that reminds me,' started Berry, 'I've been meaning to ask you about something... something about the party... '

'Yes?'

'Well, I've been wondering, Grethe, why was it that you kept claiming to be Russian?'

'Oh! For a moment there, I thought you were going to ask why I led you to my room that night!'

Grethe noticed that Berry was tapping his cigarette ash into a hole in the wooden desktop and considered it strange; she wondered where the ashes would land.

'Sorry?' he replied with a puzzled look upon his face, for evidently not knowing or at least, not remembering the incident to which she was referring. 'What do you mean?'

In place of knowing what to say, Grethe closely examined the jacket lying across her lap, before promptly pushing her finger through the tear and making it worse. She did not know why she was about to tell a lie. She knew that in truth, she had deliberately encouraged Berry to her room after the party. She knew that she had wanted some careless attention; that she had needed to feel less disorientated; that she had been seeking some warmth in her room to replace the missing curtains; that she had simply forgotten all about her father sleeping in there.

'Erm… you *followed* me to my room at the end of the night,' she explained, 'but my father was in there and you were really drunk, so I turned you away at the door. Do you not remember this at all, Berry?'

'No, not at all, but that's okay,' Berry responded, indifferently, before getting up to look for something in the wardrobe.

'And as for the Russian thing, well, I don't know why I acted like that,' she added. 'I was drunk and had only moved in here earlier that day. I guess I didn't know what I was doing.'

Everything and nothing could be explained by being

drunk. But it appeared that Berry was no longer paying much attention anyway; for some reason, he was more concerned with sifting through the clothes that were hanging in the wardrobe.

'Here, look!' he finally said, as he turned to her and held up two crumpled jackets. 'As it turns out, you're not alone… '

Grethe smiled: there were small tears in the upper arms that were almost identical to her own.

'My room is down on the fifth floor,' she suggested, 'I have some alcohol there. I suggest we go and share it… '

*

As he peered back at her over the bottle, Berry Walker commented that the taste of cheap, sugary wine reminded him of Christmas dinners; of the small-talk around the family table; of the dry bird that always got stuck in his stepfather's throat.

Grethe closed the door and turned off the main light, leaving the room in just the low shades of the bedside lamp. The sounds of her neighbour, Catrina Bloodly, talking and watching television were seeping through the wall. She sat down on her bed and kicked off her shoes, sending each spinning to different corners. She was then handed the bottle, which her father had left there days earlier by mistake, wrapped in a plastic bag on one of her shelves.

On her chin, Grethe felt a tiny trail of red that had escaped from her lips and wiped it away with the back of her hand. She lay down and rested her head upon the pillows. Glancing along the length of her body, she located Berry; he was kneeling near her feet, resting his arms upon the shallow ledge beneath the windows and looking out through the glass. From the angle she was smiling at him, he looked almost hidden, for there was only a small portion of his face that was not being shrouded by his long, dark hair. He looked like he was engaged in serious thought and as if his figure was blending with the surrounding shadows.

'What are you thinking about?'

Reaching into her handbag, which she had thrown onto the bedside chair, Grethe found a cigarette and lit it. She passed it to Berry and observed how it illuminated areas of his face in patches of flickering light. She anticipated his answer:

'Nothing.'

Grethe smiled, straightened the white bedcovers and, with a nudge from one foot, regained his attention.

'Mm... I'm tired... ' she mumbled, as she slid underneath the bedcovers, which felt tight against her body, because Berry was on top of the other half. 'How about you?'

He lay down beside her, but did not respond. He was looking up, perhaps at the smoke, which was rising and interweaving in the light from the bedside lamp.

Quietly beneath the bedcovers, and trying not to make it too obvious that she was doing so, Grethe slowly began to slide off her dress. She edged it down from her shoulders and along her body, then lifted her legs out through the top. Then, after bundling it together, she dropped it over the side of the bed.

Reaching over him, she squashed the finished cigarette into the small china ashtray she kept upon the window ledge and continued, carefully: 'Are you... are you not tired?'

Berry propped himself up on his elbows and then, in a voice only just loud enough not to be considered a whisper, finally replied, 'Why? Do you want me to go? If you're tired do you...'

Grethe shook her head: it made him stop. She looked up at the old photographs she had placed on the wall above the bed and paused to consider things. And then, by catching sight of those images, set against her otherwise empty wall, in her otherwise colourless room, Grethe realised that she felt more disorientated than she ever had before.

With the bedcovers barely covering her body, she sat up and turned to Berry.

'Well, *Mr. Walker*,' she said, as suggestively as she could without feeling too embarrassed, 'I'll just have to *make you* tired then… '

*

Ring! Ring!

…

Ring! Ring!

…

Impulsively, Grethe threw her arm toward the bedside table. The room was filled with bright sunlight. She lifted her head from Berry Walker's chest and for a moment felt unsure of where she was. She then saw his shoes – one stained oddly red – lying upside down beside the bed. The last thing she remembered was falling asleep with her arm draped over Berry and, in place of the dull waves of the television through the wall, there being silence, almost completely.

Ring! Ring!

…

Ring! Ring!

…

'It's okay,' she remembered Berry say, 'you can go to sleep. I don't mind.'

But Grethe had not wanted to fall asleep and had tried not to close her eyes.

'But Berry, you won't sleep,' she remembered herself slurring back. 'You are an insomniac. It's like midday to you now... '

She remembered how entirely relaxed she had felt in the stillness, in the absence of knowing what to say. She remembered her eyelids becoming heavy and how, by almost closing them, Berry's image had been reduced to a blurry outline through her eyelashes. She remembered how there had no longer been any uncertainty, or indecision, or tension between her and the body against which she had laid. She remembered how all she had wanted to do was to stay awake with him, for as long as the softness of the bed had allowed her to.

She remembered trying to revive a conversation and how whenever he had replied, she had felt his words vibrating through his chest:

'So, Berry, I've heard you want to be a writer... '

'Really? Who told you that?'

'Molly told me so earlier, over a glass of wine or two.'

'Oh.'

She remembered Berry reaching up to discard a finished cigarette and, in showing some apparent awkwardness, accidentally pressing it into the window ledge itself, rather than the ashtray.

'Perhaps someday, Berry, you will write about me... '

Grethe remembered how thereafter, she had quietly laid there feeling confident, at ease and comfortable with her ability to stay awake with him for hours longer into the night.

The very next thing she remembered after that was waking up...

Ring! Ring!

'I'm sorry,' she said, 'please don't wake up... '

Ring! Ring!

...

Finally, Grethe found the telephone and stopped the noise abruptly:

Ring! Ri...

She lifted the receiver and pressed it against her ear. She already knew who would be calling.

'Hei!' she greeted, *'Mitä kuuluu?'*

She looked at Berry; he was sitting upright, a grey figure against the sunlight.

'Todella mukava kuulla ääntäsi.'

She watched as he shuffled over to the edge of the bed, his eyes hidden behind his messy hair.

'Minulle kuuluu hyvää. Kaikki on kunnossa.'

As she listened to the distant voice at the other end of the telephone, Grethe began to feel a flush of red across her cheeks. It was uncomfortable: the call had come too early. So she quickly thought of a lie, an excuse for her to end the conversation:

'Olen pahoillani, mutta nyt ei ole hyvä aika puhua. Minulla on vähän kiire. Voinko soittaa sinulle myöhemmin takaisin?'

She would return the call later that morning, after Berry had gone, when she would be confused and unsure about how she felt. She would return the call because acting like normal, pretending as if nothing had changed, would seem like the easiest thing to do.

'Jutellaan pian uudestaan,' she said, before replacing the telephone to the bedside table. *'Minulla on ikävä sinua... '*

And from the telephone she heard the same, as if it were an echo:

'Minulla on ikävä sinua... Rakastan sinua... Ikävöin sinua...'

8

Logan Waters, surrounded by the litter left by recent visitors, was lying on his bed watching television, when Berry Walker entered his room. Berry had just left Grethe's sketchbook outside of her door, before retreating along the hallway. With his empty bag swinging in one hand, he crossed Logan's room with care; there were open paint tins on the floor and wet canvases leaning against the walls. With an outstretched foot, Logan stabbed at the television and it went quiet.

Shortly, Berry heard the sound of a door opening, followed by familiar shoes rustling against the hallway carpet.

'Hello!' Logan exclaimed, sitting up. 'Come in and join us… '

Berry turned in his seat: Grethe had appeared in the open doorway. She looked pleased with the messy page he had written in her sketchbook, he thought.

Logan added: 'Pull up a chair… '

But Grethe shook her head: she was on her way upstairs to visit Molly Colour, she said. As she waved goodbye, Berry noticed that she was holding a folded sheet of paper in her hand, the contents of which he was unable to see.

'By the way,' she asked, as she withdrew from the doorframe, 'where did you go this morning, Berry?'

*

The next day, in the afternoon, Berry Walker was mindlessly watching the television that stood at the foot of Logan Waters' bed. It was mesmerising. Logan was snoring; mixed visions of shampoo, canned laughter, explosions and biscuits had caused him to fall asleep.

Outside it was raining heavily. All day, rainwater had been flowing down the sides of the building and draping the windows. As another movie started, Berry felt full of stale toast and black coffee and boredom. He had been flicking between channels and staring into the glow for too long.

… A man and a woman are sitting together. It has been a long journey and they are both looking forward to getting home. There is a storm outside and every so often, lightning is causing the small window beside them to flash white…

I, meanwhile, was descending the stairwell. From a leak in the roof, strings of water were plunging down the central shaft and splattering loudly on the distant ground. I was spinning borrowed keys on my finger.

… A stewardess walks past in a hurry. She is wearing blue clothes and has brown hair. The man tries to gain her attention, but he is ignored.

The window flashes white again. The man is afraid of flying and the woman is holding his hand…

Logan's snoring was getting louder. To quieten him, Berry reached over and pushed him over onto his side. Then, having heard the stairwell door open, he turned around:

'Well, Jamie, did you get the bottle?' he asked. 'It was on top of my desk, where you left it yesterday by mistake… '

I returned to my seat and threw his keys over to him. He asked me if I had locked his room behind me, but I pretended not to hear him.

… And the man and the woman both try to relax. (Flash!) And they both recline in their seats. (Flash!) And they both close their eyes. (Flash!) And they are both completely unaware of the sheer panic in the cockpit…

Impulsively, Berry turned off the television and for a second or two the black screen fizzled. In the sudden absence of lightning and aeroplanes, silence fell sharply upon the room and Berry began to detect a distinctive sound: it was Grethe's telephone; it was ringing two rooms away.

He grabbed the bottle that had been retrieved from his room, opened it and slumped back into the chair. He despised that telephone. He despised the way in which it would erupt without warning. He despised having to listen to, but not understand, Grethe's Finnish conversations. He despised how, in an unknown context, he could often hear his own name being used.

Berry took a large swig from the bottle.

And the ringing continued… and the ringing continued…

'Do you hear that, Jamie?' he finally asked. 'Why isn't she answering *his* call?'

I said nothing. Evidently, Berry had failed to notice Grethe creeping past the open doorway and into the stairwell minutes earlier…

15

To distract herself from having conflicting thoughts, Annelie Strandli, sitting at one end of the dining table in her parents' house, laughed at a joke and covered her mouth, in case the food she was chewing escaped from it. Whenever she had been away in Finland, the secret story, and the possibility of her finding new additions to it, had seldom crossed her mind. In his kiss, if only for short moments, Gunnar had always been able to reduce the hidden text to a passing triviality, to a casual curiosity that was willingly forgotten, but not with Berry Walker sitting at the other end of the table. She looked across at him, wanting to catch his eye, only to find that he was busy discussing something with her mother.

With great fondness Grethe recalled how, earlier that day, she had come to discover the final piece of the story. It had been in the morning, just before their flight together to Finland when, having gone up to his room to wake him, she had found Berry's door left wide open and his bed left unused. It had surprised her to find his desk unlocked, for although she had been obsessively checking it whenever possible, it had not been so for nearly two months. She had sat down and then, with the papers shaking in her hands, read through the last part until she had reached its end:

… Over time, with discipline and belief, Boy One would succeed in gaining the control he desired over his dreams. Each and every day, he would close his eyes, concentrate upon the image he had created and then casually dream with She by his side, until eventually the ritual could be observed automatically. And so for thousands of nights (and for as many daylight hours as possible) throughout his teenage years, She would be part of the scenery, of the furniture, during every scenario that Boy One would ever dream.

He would always remember that morning in Old Man's shop and how relieved he had felt, knowing that his internal crisis had been resolved. He would remember how Old Man, after having sat there listening, had only wanted to ask the same question as before:

'So, what about Love?'

Old Man had agreed that through his creation, She, Boy One had managed to resolve his fear of Death. However, he had also believed that it would prove useless against the other great perplexity of life: Love. He had explained that in his view, whilst Death could be challenged with an act of creation, Love always required something more to be resolved: an act of expression.

'Take my writing, for example,' he had illustrated. 'For me, my writing helps me to defeat the uncertainty of Death. And yet, other than that, my writing serves little purpose – hell, it doesn't even exist! – until it has been read, until it has been expressed and received, until it has been given life within the mind of its reader. Likewise, there is little purpose served by being in love until the fact is known by the object of its desire… '

Not long after that morning, one night in his sleep and with a curious smile upon his face, Old Man would die. Boy One would never again speak to anyone about She. He would always fantasise about his friend's final moments on Earth, about how he must have spent them standing at the edge of a cliff, staring down at his own body and wishing that She had been there to wake him.

'... what I'm trying to say is, do not become so concerned with Death that you forget all about Love. For Love, after all, is the means by which we are able to live.'

Six

As Boy One grew older, the image of She evolved in tandem with his changing thoughts and aspirations, until one day, She was no longer there at all. It happened unexpectedly, on a day that seemed no different to any other, in the office where he worked years later. It happened in a brief moment, a moment he had always known might occur, but had never dared to believe.

In his office job, Boy One was charged with the task of arranging forgettable papers into forgettable piles. The office was situated at the top of a tall building with a broken elevator. Once he had climbed the countless staircases and reached his desk, he did not mind the work; it was undemanding enough for his mind to wander elsewhere. The desks were lined in long rows and surrounded by raised partitions that separated each from the others. Boy One's desk was at the far corner of the room, allowing him to enjoy quick, air-conditioned dreams with She whenever he pleased.

The interior of his dream was clouded with grey. Everything looked familiar, although nothing was quite the same; the shapes were without structure; the edges were without lines. A bird flew backwards past the window. A stack of papers lurched toward him, only to dissolve into the air. A computer buzzed and shuddered, as its pixels broke free of the screen. There were cut up voices coming from the radio. There were lines of binary code on his desk, and a rolled up banknote for him to snort them.

'I want everyone's attention... I want everyone's attention right now!'

Boy One lifted his head from his desk and shook himself to wake up. He hated dreaming about work; it offered little of the escapism he had wanted to achieve.

'I said RIGHT NOW!'

It was his supervisor: he was shouting from the other side of the office. Boy One sat up in his seat, just high enough to peer over the partitions. The supervisor, who was a fat and dominating man, was perched on top of the photocopier, causing it to creak under the strain. He began addressing the workers who had left their desks and were gathering around. Boy One watched from a distance, being careful not to be seen. The supervisor was introducing a new employee, someone hidden behind the crowd. Boy One shuffled from side to side until finally, through a momentary gap between two people, he was able to see.

Shocked, he slumped back down and spun around. His head fell forward and struck the keyboard, sending strings of letters across the screen. In the background, the supervisor's voice subsided and the crowd dispersed. He ignored everything. He was in disbelief. Never before had he failed to distinguish the difference between being awake and asleep.

'WHAT DO YOU THINK YOU'RE DOING?'

Boy One looked up and felt the imprint of the keyboard upon his cheek. The supervisor was standing over him.

'WHY DIDN'T YOU COME OVER WITH THE OTHERS?'

Boy One did not answer. He stared at the supervisor, whose face was flushed with red and who had a jagged vein running down his forehead.

'YOU'RE WASTING MY TIME, MAKING ME COME OVER HERE LIKE THIS,' the supervisor continued, before lowering his voice and gesturing to the person standing beside him: 'Anyway, I was just introducing everyone to the newest member of our team. This is… '

'Stop,' Boy One interrupted him. 'I already know who she is.'

'You… you do?'

'Of course I do! She was supposed to have woken me up by now!'

'WHAT?' the supervisor raised his voice again, only louder than before, causing the blue vein to throb like it was about to burst. 'WHAT DID YOU SAY?'

Boy One spun around in his chair and laughed, 'I hate dreaming about work, don't you? What I wouldn't give now for a black cat riding a bicycle… '

'WHAT…WHAT ARE YOU TALKING ABOUT?'

'Listen, I know I'm still asleep,' he smiled. 'I knew it from the very moment that She showed up… '

Boy One returned his head to the keyboard and looked away. The supervisor stormed off, leaving him alone with nothing but the sound of the computer's bleeps and moans. He grinned to himself, but something was not quite right; She had seemed different somehow. He glanced to the window and suddenly froze. His blood rushed away from his head, leaving him feeling pale and faint. He stared through the glass in disbelief: outside it was a beautiful day, and all of the birds were flying forward.

That night, for the first time in his life, when Boy One slept he did not dream. The appearance of the girl in the office, who looked as identical to She as it was possible to be, had unravelled his creation at the seams. He woke up long before dawn, not knowing where he had just been. The rest of the night was dark, but in the morning the sunshine was brighter than he had ever seen.

He had come to understand what Old Man had meant about Love. The sense of chaos he was feeling could not be resolved by thoughts and theories alone, but rather through the means of expression that he felt most comfortable with: Literature. He would write everything down and over time it would all come together: of his dreaming, of his fears, of his teacher's malice, of She and of Death, of Old Man's tired words, and of all the sentiments he would feel desperate to have revealed. And each time he would finish writing a piece, he would leave it in a secret place for the girl to read, and then watch from afar as his thoughts were expressed and received.

(THE END)

*

Ever since the beginning of the story, Grethe had looked forward to the end. She had always believed that without an ending, without a point of resolution, without a moment against which the beginning and everything that had followed could be gauged, she might find no meaning in it at all. And yet, after having finally reached its end, Grethe had realised that all along, the purpose of the story was for something simple and obvious, something that she had known from the start, something that she had not wanted to admit to herself: it was a declaration of the writer's love for his reader.

Later that night, as she was lying in a basement bed with Gunnar sleeping by her side, Grethe found that for the first time ever, she was completely incapable of falling asleep. With darkness the surroundings and Gunnar's heavy breathing the soundtrack, she had become lost in thoughts regarding Berry Walker; it felt as if his details were satellites orbiting her memory. Earlier, Berry had retired from her family's dining table long before anyone else. He had looked tired and bemused. She recalled how early that morning in London, soon after having replaced the story to its familiar hiding place, she had found him asleep in one of Logan Waters' seats.

Grethe wrestled a few more inches of the bedcovers away from Gunnar. Then she started to think again about the story and about why, up to that point, Berry had still never spoken about, or presented it to her. She realised that if, in mimicking his own fiction, the writer had really designed the story to be a means of expressing the otherwise inexpressible, to be a channel through which he could comfortably reach her, then it would have failed in its purpose if it were not revealed. After all, she thought, a declaration of love, regardless of how it comes to be delivered, is no declaration at all until it is expressed and received.

… And I, meanwhile in my room, had removed my ear from a wall that I no longer needed to hear through.

Impulsively, Grethe quickly sat up in the bed, causing Gunnar to stir. Everything was suddenly clear: the writer had already revealed the story to her. He had been gradually doing so ever since they had first met. Of all the times she had looked inside his desk, she had never been doing so in secret. The writer, she realised, had been leaving the pages there with the intention of her finding them. He had been purposely leaving the desk unlocked at times when he had known she would be alone with it. All along, of all the quiet exchanges between the writer and the reader through that old wooden desk, there had been no real secrets; like so much else between them, it had just been another matter they had felt unwilling to speak about. And yet, through this unsaid process of hiding and seeking, the story had mutually served both its writer and its reader: through it the writer had expressed to the reader all that he had wished to express, whilst the reader had received the greater understanding of the writer she had sought.

Grethe lay back down and then, even though she knew that she and Berry would never speak about the story, and even though she knew that after he had left Finland she would never see him again, started to feel an uncontrollable urge to smile. In comfort, she began to fall asleep and as she did so, concentrated upon the image she most wanted to dream. She pictured a house in the country, a house within which Berry Walker could be found sitting. She pictured a window that opened out onto green hills, a window through which a soft wind could be felt blowing. She pictured a desk that was old, a desk before which her writer could be glimpsed working. She pictured typed pages that were lying in a pile, pages across which unknown words could be seen running.

… And I, meanwhile in my room, had discarded a small rusty key that I no longer needed to use.

(THE END)

LUKE BITMEAD BURSARY

The award was set up shortly after Luke's death in 2006 by his family to support and encourage the work of fledgling novel writers. The top prize is a publishing contract with Legend Press, as well as a cash bursary.

We are delighted to be working with Luke's family to ensure that Luke's name and memory lives on – not only through his work, but through this wonderful memorial bursary too. For those of you lucky enough to have met Luke you will know that he was hugely compassionate and would love the idea of another struggling talented writer being supported on the arduous road to securing their first publishing deal.

We will ensure that, as with all our authors, we give the winner of the bursary as much support as we can, and offer them the most effective creative platform from which to showcase their talent. We can't wait to start reading and judging the submissions.

We are pleased to be continuing this brilliant bursary for a fifth year, and hope to follow in the success of our previous winners Andrew Blackman (*On the Holloway Road*, February 2009), Ruth Dugdall (*The Woman Before Me*, August 2010) Sophie Duffy (*The Generation Game*, August 2011) and J.R. Crook (*Sleeping Patterns*, July 2012).

For more information on the bursary, visit:
www.legendpress.co.uk

Come and visit us at

www.legendpress.co.uk

www.twitter.com/legend_press

www.jrcrook.co.uk

www.twitter.com/jrcrookkk

Lightning Source UK Ltd.
Milton Keynes UK
UKOW050117040712

195412UK00001B/4/P